Sex, Lies and Drama

FIRE
&
BRIMSTONE

Sex, Lies and Drama

FIRE
&
BRIMSTONE

Laurinda D. Brown

A STREBOR BOOKS INTERNATIONAL LLC PUBLICATION
DISTRIBUTED BY SIMON & SCHUSTER, INC.

Published by

Strebor Books International LLC
P.O. Box 1370
Bowie, MD 20718
http://www.streborbooks.com

ISBN 1-59309-015-3
LCCN 2003105034

Distributed by Simon & Schuster, Inc.
1230 Avenue of the Americas
New York, NY 10020
1-800-223-2336

First Printing March 2004
Manufactured and Printed in the United States

10 9 8 7 6 5 4 3

Dedicated to the loving memory of
Ms. Shirley Ann Pilcher Brown
July 1950 – May 2000

"I love you, Momma, and miss you tremendously. With everything that has happened in my life, I can finally say that it has all come full circle, and while counting my many blessings, I now know that 'I got myself some meaning.'"

A Word from the Author

When I decided to do a book on homosexuality and religion,
I knew that other issues were going to be addressed because that's
just how life is. Those issues are actually more important than
an individual's religious or sexual preference. Single or married,
the bills still have to be paid, and the children must be fed.
Baptist or Catholic, the Bible still reads the same, and we serve
the same God. Gay or straight, Black or White, one must
learn self-acceptance—if you don't like you, who else will?

"Upon the wicked He shall rain snares; fire and brimstone, and horrible tempest; this shall be the portion of their cup."

Psalm 11:6

RELIGION IS FOR THOSE WHO
ARE AFRAID TO GO TO HELL

"For this cause God gave them up into vile affections;
for even their women did change the natural use into that which is
against nature: And the likewise also the men, leaving the natural
use of the woman, burned in their lust one toward another;
men with men working that which is unseemly, and receiving
in themselves that recompense of their error which was meet."

Romans 1:26-27

1

"Why do you start this shit every Sunday morning!" Gayle screamed as she stormed out of the bedroom. She slammed the door so hard the dresser mirror shook, and all of the cards and pictures that were stuck in the crevices fell to the surface.

Gayle was a beautiful, big-boned woman. She had an ass that any man would damn near kill for and plenty of breasts to go along with it. Her voluptuous lips were perfectly shaped, for they were soft and tasted like strawberries, even at the break of dawn. Her silky-smooth, milk-chocolate skin was blemish-free and had a glow that could light up any room. She kept her hair cut stylishly low, and it was extremely becoming on her rounded, fat face. Sexy would never be enough to describe her eyes. They were the prettiest shade of brown, and, whenever she sang with the melodious voice that God had blessed her with, those gorgeous eyes crooned to her lover's heart whether the song was R&B, jazz, or gospel.

"What are you talking about, Gayle?" Chris mumbled into the pillow. "You get up every Sunday bitchin' about something."

"Me?" Gayle snapped as she tugged on her pantyhose. Besides having sex, putting on her pantyhose every Sunday morning was the only exercise that she got. "You're the one who gets such a 'tude on Sunday mornings when I get up to go to church. You start throwin' shit and acting like you're possessed or something. You come up with every reason in the world why I shouldn't take the car out. You've flattened the tires. You…"

"Wait a minute," Chris answered. "I didn't flatten those tires. You always blame shit like that on me." The pillow was pulled tighter with the intent of drowning out yet another argument.

"Anyway, Chris, I'm tired of this. When I start puttin' on my clothes, you get this attitude with me that lasts until 12:01 Monday morning. I mean it's like clockwork."

Gayle got up and went into the bathroom and started putting on her makeup. These arguments had become pretty regular, and there seemed to be no end to them. With each passing Sunday, they had become worse, and on this particular Sunday, Gayle knew that it would be a turning point in their relationship. As she stroked her red makeup sponge across her forehead, she leaned around the corner and glared at Chris.

"Question," she said, pausing to complete her last stroke.

"What?"

Gayle came out of the bathroom and took a seat on the edge of the bed. "Why is it that you always want to have sex before I leave to go to church? First, you won't let me touch you on Saturday nights, but then you wanna get up the next morning and go at it like a dog in heat. The only thing on my mind is going to church. I have to go to church, and you know that. You know the responsibilities that I have on Sunday mornings, but you're so dead set on trying to get you some ass. And you just ain't right for that."

Chris didn't answer.

"You hear me talkin' to you?"

Gayle got up and walked to Chris' side of the bed. She reached for the hand that was delicately placed on top of the smooth, beige body that she had grown to love more than she had ever loved any before. Chris pulled away from her and sat straight up in the bed, giving Gayle a look that appeared painful but sincere. Gayle was incensed with Chris, but she could also see the sadness in Chris' eyes.

"Chris, baby, what's wrong with you? Why do we go through this every week? There's got to be something more to this. I feel like there's something going on with you that you don't want me to know about. Aren't you tired of all the fighting?" She got up and looked out the window, noticing how bright the sun was. It was a perfect day for a stroll in the park with her family after church. "Hey, I have an idea. Why don't you come to church with me? Afterwards, we can go to the park or something."

"You're kiddin', right?"

"No, I'm not. I'm serious this time. It might do us some good."

"You actually think that me going to church with you is going to make everything all right? It's like you sleep with me Monday through Saturday but then, come Sunday, it's a sin and a shame." Chris chuckled, pushing back against the brass headboard. "Answer me this one question, Gayle."

"Sure, baby. Anything."

"How in the hell can you go to church on Sunday mornings and minister to a congregation of nearly a thousand people when you just got out of bed with a woman?"

Gayle's mouth dropped open, and tears filled the wells of her eyes. She realized that she had no answer for that question.

2

Later that Sunday morning, Chris sat outside on the patio and watched the ducks and their ducklings waddle down the walkway. There was a lake behind the apartment that she and Gayle shared and, on Sunday mornings, sitting outside watching her white neighbors walking with their children calmed her tremendously. Each one of them seemed trouble-free, walking with straight backs and heads held high. Southern white folks had a rhythm about them that didn't need any music—the kind of rhythm that let the world believe that you were all that and a bag of chips when you really were more broke than a po' man on welfare and frequently robbed Peter to pay Paul; the kind of rhythm that echoed the reminder that no matter how many times they dined with Black folks and cheered for each other's children at sporting events, that infamous "We're still better than you" attitude kept them mentally, culturally and, most times, socially separated from their Black neighbors. It was a rhythm that Black folks sometimes ridiculed but often found comfort in. Even with dual Bachelor's degrees in French and English from Howard University—the Black Mecca of Higher Education—coupled with her abundant good looks, Chris, at this moment in time, didn't have that rhythm. She couldn't get it even if she'd tried, and, for all that her life should have been right then, it was extraordinarily frustrating. The pressure of being without an air of confidence was killing her on the inside.

Mark Mason, their next-door neighbor, was a tall, middle-aged white man who had done an excellent job of minding his business. He never seemed to have any female guests over, but he did have quite a few male visitors of different social and racial persuasions. Chris knew that he'd heard some of the recent vicious fights between Gayle and her. On one night in particular, Gayle threw a toddler car seat at Chris, and, if she hadn't ducked, Chris' head would have been smashed in. The seat actually ended up hitting the wall that separated the two apartments. And just two days before, the property manager had sent a nice-nasty note saying that the lady who lived in the apartment on the other side of them had complained of hearing screaming and fighting almost every other night. "Either calm down the noise and activity or move." The note was embarrassing but true. The two of them could not continue to live like this.

In spite of the fact that she absolutely detested Memphis, Chris had regrettably returned to her hometown to give birth to the child conceived with her college sweetheart, Trey Withers. Within that first year of being seemingly condemned to eternal unhappiness, she had grown terribly lonely and resented the fact that she no longer had access to the openness of the "life" as it was lived in Washington, D.C.

To explore her curiosities in Memphis, Chris would have to be inconspicuous, hiding her alternative newspapers and maintaining a proper number of male acquaintances while, at the same time, relishing in the newness of motherhood. To her, Memphis was not the place to be gay or to even think about it. There was just too many "toos" about it. There were too many eyes on her at home and far too many people who knew her. At church she could never feel comfortable because, as a church scholarship recipient, the expectations were too many and too far beyond her reach. It was too difficult for her to sit in a pew while she craved for the flesh of a woman. Instead, while in Memphis—a metropolis in its own right, Chris tended to deny her desire for women and that was the reason she so desperately had wanted to stay away in the first place.

Memphis, Tennessee: a big, small town full of small talk from people with little minds and big mouths, and Chris knew that this was way beyond her tolerance. Most of the people that she'd gone to high school with did exactly what Chris had done. They left Memphis with all intent of never returning, and that they did... every last one of them. So when she returned, Chris' homecoming lacked the fanfare of missed acquaintances and childhood friends wanting to get together to catch up on each other's lives. Those classmates and friends left behind weren't interested in reminiscing with the fat, smart girl whose thighs rubbed together and dressed from Lane Bryant and Roaman's—back when you could only get their clothes from the catalog. That was also the time when clothes any larger than size 16 were sold in the Budget Career section of the department store where everything had elastic in the waist.

She often found herself invited to house parties only when some of her so-called "cool" friends needed someone's mother to drive them there. Cool but stupid, none of them realized that Chris knew what was going on. As soon as she was able, Chris would sneak to a phone to summon her mother while everyone else was trying to get their groove on. "So and so's daddy is coming to get them," Chris would lie. "I wanted to wait on you." Mrs. Desmereaux, tired but always yearning for her older daughter to loosen up and live a little, got up from her bed to go get her. Although Chris had a midnight curfew, she was never out past eleven.

Entering Howard University in the late 80's, Chris found herself dumbfounded by the number of beautiful African-American women on campus. She realized soon thereafter that there was something inside of her that was trying to break free. Granted, her beautiful smile and honey-bronzed skin mesmerized every man she'd ever met. She had shark-like eyes, dark but filled with a brilliance that had touched the lives of many. Her kisses were always exceptionally succulent because the fullness within her lips held a moisture only found in early morning dew.

For as long as Chris could remember, her father had teased her about having "caint-dontya" hair. In English, that translated to "can't comb it and don't you try." Sitting in the beauty shop on Saturday mornings was a family tradition that Chris couldn't wait to break. She hated the four-hundred degree heat of the dryer and detested the smell of the hot comb. As she tearfully sat there in what seemed to be the most ragged salon chair in the world, for year Chris endured what she thought to be almost barbaric torture. Miss Mildred, the busty hairdresser with the horn-rimmed glasses, didn't care that the hot comb was too hot or that she'd burned Chris' ear with dripping, hot pressing oil.

By junior high school, Chris started getting perms because Ms. Desmereaux had grown tired of fighting with her when it was time to comb her hair. And to save Chris from her father's constant teasing, Miss Mildred got paid before anybody. But now, some one thousand miles away from the only person who'd ever permed her hair, Chris was faced with the dilemma of do-it-yourself perms because there was no way that she'd ever be able to afford the sixty dollars and up fees for a D.C. hairdresser. Every touchup was a trial and error period, with Chris eventually losing hair due to over-processing and hot curlers. Soon she'd opted to just cut it off and start over. Fortunately, Chris found a person in her dormitory with just enough cosmetology training to help her grow a healthy head of reddish-brown hair for only five dollars a sitting. Her clothes might not have always fit, nor was she ever the richest girl on campus, but her cleanliness and zest for having "just a little bit more" made her company a pleasure and her conversation fulfilling.

Despite a well-rounded group of cultured, straight girlfriends, Chris still felt an overwhelming desire to amass alternative news-papers and search through the "Women seeking Women" section of the classifieds. Answering an ad was off-limits. "Look but don't touch." However, language in the personal ads alone had a tendency to be intriguing.

On her weekends off, Chris strolled through the neighborhood around 17th and P Streets hoping to catch a glimpse of a proud, beautiful, and professional gay woman who used discretion when seeking pleasurable company. Dupont Circle, located in the heart of the gay and lesbian district, played host to Chris' need to be surrounded by those like her—those who had a secret which, like a tulip, only blossomed when the climate was favorable. Otherwise, it remained dormant. Curvaceous busts, waists, and backsides of any woman enticed Chris but failed to arouse her. The look of a woman's foot delicately raised in a pair of two-inch heels made those thoughts even more pleasant.

That's nasty, she'd think to herself. I ain't supposed to be thinking like this.

Having been raised in a culture that was not accustomed to giving compliments—only senseless and sometimes heartless criticism—Chris soon understood that there was nothing wrong with an admiration for being feminine...for just being a lady. Therefore, Chris believed that her sensations would dissolve in time. Whenever there were no male suitors in search of a midnight booty call, Chris knew one thing: she wished to love a woman the way her father had not, to love a woman the way she deserved to be loved—the way her father could not. But to fight that feeling, however, in a society still not ready to accept the love between two people of the same sex, Chris kept male company—even when she didn't want it.

That gay woman that Chris most needed to acknowledge, accept and learn to love greeted her in the mirror every morning and slumbered inside her soul every night. With all of that noted but tucked away, Chris openly pursued what was the norm; never considering the damage to all others involved or herself.

With thoughts of the many women that her father had simultaneously romanced echoing through her mind, Chris was determined to never allow such treatment from a man. Her belief was that you should love one and only one. Trying to love two people at the same time wasn't right, nor was it fair. Chris learned to combine her sympathy for the many disrespected women in her father's life with her own compassion and desire to love. Her heart overflowing with so much to give, Chris never bothered to protect herself from the brutal reality of rejection and heartache. Instead, she embraced the world around her and adjusted herself, as needed—even when it came to relationships.

From Trinidad to Los Angeles, thousands of beautiful, strong Black men and women had come to Howard in search of the same thing: a chance to become somebody. Howard's social history had its reputation to protect, and the abundance of parties and prestigious alumni helped the university live up to that reputation. Any woman fortunate enough to get her hands on a good man, a Howard one or not, held on to him but, in the absence of that, Howard women relied heavily on the bond of friendship with one another.

Freshman orientation introduced Chris to her first real friend, Darcy—short for Darcyne Elizabeth Anderson. She was the daughter of a 70's disco singer who, along with his band, had met an untimely death in a plane crash two weeks after she was born. Their only record went gold the next day and platinum the next month and Darcy, as his sole heir, was financially set for life. But her mother, Elsa Anderson, was a conservative woman who had taught her daughter the importance of making a name for herself and not to rely on the memory of her father for a lifetime of free and easy rides. With that advice in tow, Darcy, while in her senior year of high school, applied for and subsequently won a merit scholarship from a wealthy Atlanta businessman. Although she didn't really need the money, Mr. Jude Edson, owner of Edson's Seafood Wharf in Atlanta, awarded her the scholarship because of her promising character and ambition. Out of boredom, Darcy took a job on the weekends at a movie theater, saving her inheritance for a rainy day.

On-campus housing was limited and, unless you knew somebody who knew somebody, it was virtually nonexistent. Living in a boarding house in Maryland during the first half of fall semester, Chris tried to make as many inroads as possible. Her commute was expensive, and it left her out of the loop when it came to campus functions and study groups. However, her assigned work-study job put her in contact with some heavy-hitters on campus who finally made calls to the Dean of Housing on Chris' behalf, and facilitated her move into the freshman dormitory a few days later. Chris made new friends but never had a lot of time to spend with them. She was swamped with two jobs and a full-time course load. As the first semester came to a close, she and Darcy had different responsibilities. Chris was trying to become somebody while Darcy struggled with forgetting who she was.

Washington, D.C.: a city providing many opportunities for all that lived there. If a person were from India or Iran, he could easily become a taxi driver—just make sure that the passengers knew how to get where they wanted to go. If from Africa or Tobago, one could set up a stand on a corner and sell oils and incense. From Korea or China? Open up a restaurant and sell what the public believed to be fine Oriental cuisine. Just hope that no one wondered why there were never any stray dogs or cats in the alleys near the establishment. Shit, there were some that had the nerve to open soul food restaurants and master cooking greens and candied yams. Their asses couldn't understand a bit of English, but when it came to taking your money, they spoke the language better than the first Pilgrim to set foot on American soil. They had the biggest sub shops and the biggest beauty supply stores in the entire city. Sistah-girls lined up for hours to get their nails done by Korean men who wore surgical masks and rubber gloves; not to protect them from the fumes or the flying acrylic but from the mere touch and smell of African-American skin.

And the politics? There was more drama than the hottest soap opera. The only difference was that the story lines and the actors were real. Hell, the mayor of the city was caught smoking crack with his ex-girlfriend, and still managed to maintain the city's respect. After going through rehab, he was able to come back and beat his replacement in the next election and serve another term.

The city afforded both Chris and Darcy many personal and social opportunities. But by the end of their sophomore year, the two of them rarely saw each other and hardly ever called. Chris had begun to tap into her "expression," devoting her free time to doing just that. Two girls she had once seen in Dupont Circle lived at the end of her hall; she avoided them like the plague. On Thursday nights, she would sneak out of the dorm and go to lesbian clubs just to be around women like her. After a couple of weeks, that activity ceased because she ran into a classmate while sitting at the bar. Not only did Chris stop going to the club, but she dropped the class also.

As she'd done the year before, Chris maintained a revolving door of men in her Meridian Hill dorm room just to keep herself occupied and her mind off other things. Her male guests were so numerous that her friends labeled her "Mistress of Seduction." Little did they know that behind those closed doors, Chris spent most of the time either watching television or doing homework on one side of the room while her "date" sat on the bed on the other side of the room. She didn't talk much unless she wanted something. No kisses, no embraces. And, if she did do anything remotely sexual, it was quick and meaningless. She never promised to phone the day after or the next and, whenever she got one of those "was it good?" follow-up calls, Chris never suppressed her true feelings and pleasantly said, "No." Anything was better than having her friends, her posse, know that she had a thing for women.

In the nation's capital, a church was on almost every corner. Any denomination you wanted—Baptist, Church of Christ, African Methodist—take your pick. With each having congregations of several hundreds, Sunday mornings were the only time cars were allowed to double-park on D.C.'s crowded streets. All of the urban radio stations played a mixture of traditional and contemporary gospel music well into the afternoon, so if you didn't feel up to taking a stroll down the aisle to sit behind the Mother Board, then you could get some good religion while driving in your car, while cleaning your house, or even while just chillin' at Bedside Baptist.

The last thing that had come out of Chris' grandmother's mouth on the day that Chris left for college was, "Make sure ya find a good church while ya up there, ya hear? Don't go ta shavin' ya head and thangs but finds ya a good church home."

Chris adored her grandmother, Albertrese Montague, who was both beautiful and wise, but Chris was sorry. Finding a church home was the last thing she wanted to do. After growing up in a house where she was forced to go to church, Chris just wasn't having it. There were Sundays when Ms. Desmereaux found herself in a brief, holy mood and insisted that her daughters accompany her to Sunday School, the morning worship service, an afternoon program, and the evening service. Chris never understood why her mother suddenly started crying one Sunday and ran to the front of the church. Chris felt embarrassed after that and protested going to church by tearing holes in her pantyhose. She was afraid that her mother was going to start falling out all over the people seated next to them and would have to be carried out by the people who dressed in white and smelled of mothballs. Everybody had a fan or made themselves one out of the program, and then they'd stand over Chris and her sister disrupting what Chris felt to be her space. She just prayed that none of them used that wad of Kleenex or that dingy handkerchief that was balled up in their pockets. Her mother would pull one of those falling-out stunts once or twice during a service, and then they might not attend church for another month. When the summer rolled around, Chris and her sister, Iysha, had to go to Vacation Bible School where the only joy Chris found was in creative arts and the refreshments. Going there wasn't a choice but an order.

To further distort what Chris was taught to respect as religion, Chris had memories of her mother's pastor coming over to Chris' aunt's house while she was growing up. He wasn't there in the broad daylight to pray or to go over Sunday School lessons. Shit, he wasn't even there to eat. He was all over Tookie—short for Tosha—the minute he hit the door, with one hand up her skirt while the other clutched and massaged her breasts. During one of his visits, Chris was trying so hard to see that she fell into the china cabinet, but they were so into it, moaning and groaning, groping and grinding, that they didn't even hear or see her.

Once she got a little older, Chris discovered that the same pastor had also had an affair with her Aunt Barbara, Tookie's older sister. He only came over at night after his wife went to work and, to keep up the image that he felt he'd earned, his dumb ass rolled up in her driveway in the brand-new Buick that the church had bought him. Dumb ass! In the years that passed, neither sibling was ashamed of her fling and, as appropriate, no one ever discussed it. What sickened Chris the most was that this was the same pastor her mother dragged her to see whenever they went to church. She detested going so much that she started tearing holes in whatever she could to keep from leaving the house. This was the same pastor who stood in the pulpit before a congregation of hundreds and preached sermon after sermon about fornication and adultery. And sadly, this was also the same pastor who ate dinner with his wife at Chris' grandmother's house every Sunday after church—with both Tookie and Barbara sitting across the table. For years, Chris, in torn clothes and all, sat on the hard pews of her personal, mental torture chamber. Through the years, she'd been made to sit enough to see cushions put on the pews.

And the fashion shows? They only got better with every member always trying to outdress the next. Sunday in and Sunday out the drama was the same. When she finally got old enough to walk out of the service without her mother's permission, Chris casually made her way to the exit during "Amazing Grace" and stayed gone until the sermon was over. In Chris' opinion, this man of God could never say anything she'd ever want to hear. Sunday night musicals performed by hip slappers from across the city; bake sales with cakes as hard as rocks and tasteless half-baked pies; and constant gossip about everything and everybody except Jesus were all parts of the "religious" experience that had been forced upon her. Growing up with that, she had no desire to find a church home. Believing that there had to be some better way to spend a Sunday, Chris found a job.

3

During their junior year, Darcy, playing matchmaker, introduced Chris to Trey. He had seen a picture of her on Darcy's wall and was dying to be introduced to the woman who always seemed to be looking back at him. As fate would have it, Trey was visiting Darcy one evening when Chris unexpectedly called.

"Darcy?" Chris' voice was very meticulous and, although they didn't talk much, Darcy immediately picked up on her voice.

"Well, ain't this nothing!" Darcy was sweet and uppity when she wanted to be, but she was still country and still had lots of Southern hospitality. That's why everybody knew it was okay to crash at her place for the weekend. She did the cooking, and everyone else brought the drinks, cards, and board games. The spades tournaments had gotten so serious that she had to rent extra card tables and chairs. There were always at least five extra decks of cards around…just in case somebody brought a friend or two. "What's up?" she shrieked. "I ain't seen you in a while."

"Honey, I've been around. Trying to get shit together for midterms. Working. Nothing really spectacular."

"I feel you on that. I saw you the other day headed across the yard, but I was in a hurry trying to get to class."

"Girl, I was probably headed home. That's a long walk at the end of a day."

"Walk? Where are you living now?"

"In this house on Second Street. Bunch of crazy ass religious folks living there, but the rent is cheap."

"Religious? You? Oh, I know yo' ass is about to go crazy."

"Yep. It's the best I can do right now, since my financial aid is still so screwed up. I hate this damn school when it comes to that. I went up there this morning to see if my loan papers had been processed. Here it is, September, and they're still talking about it's an eight-week process."

"Chris, it's just the middle of September."

"They've had the shit since last spring, Darcy. C'mon now."

"Aw, well, that's different."

"The trifling ho that's supposed to be helping me walked past me eating a fuckin' hot dog and rolled her eyes at me. When I got into her office, she acted like she didn't know what the hell I was there for. She sees me almost twice a week, and each time I have to refresh her memory about the situation. Same ol' Howard bullshit. You're so lucky that you don't have to put up with that."

By this time, Chris could hear commotion in the background, and realized that Darcy had been distracted for quite some time. Whoever it was wanted to talk to Chris. Darcy cuffed the receiver, muffling her conversation.

Whispering, Darcy said, "Look, there's this guy over here that's been bugging me about meeting you, and he just realized that I'm talking to you…"

The handset was snatched from Darcy's hands, and Chris could hear her fighting to get it back.

"Who dis?" the husky voice asked. "Is dis Darcy's niggah?"

"Excuse me?" Chris responded. The voice's owner was giggling like a young schoolboy and, at that moment, Chris didn't have time for games. "May I please speak back to Darcy?" she demanded.

Realizing that the other party was obviously female, he asked, "Are you the girl in the picture?"

"What picture?"

"The picture hanging on the wall in Darcy's room."

The voice had matured a little bit and had regained some composure.

"What does it look like?"

Chris couldn't remember any picture that she'd given Darcy and was absolutely clueless.

Right then, Chris heard the receiver hit the floor.

"Aw, shit, it is her! C'mon, Darcy, hook me up!"

Chris started blushing.

Out of breath, Darcy snatched the phone back. "Girl, I'm sorry. That was Trey. We can discuss him later. What did you need?"

"I called to see if you'd kept any notes from Dr. Hill's class. We've got a test next week, and I'm missing a few things. You know how I tend to miss class every now and then."

"Every now and then? I know better than that shit. Hell, knowing you, it was too cold to get out of bed, and you decided to miss class. But, yeah, I've got all of his stuff. Want me to meet you on campus tomorrow with it? I've got some work to do in the psych department in the morning. We can hook up there or in Blackburn, since I need to go to the bookstore."

"Blackburn is too far. I'll meet you in the psych department."

"That's cool. Is nine-thirty good for you?"

"Yeah, I'll see you then."

Darcy covered the receiver again and whispered, "I'll call you back when he leaves."

"Okay."

About three hours later, Darcy called and gave Chris the lowdown on Trey. It was after midnight but Chris, intrigued by all the attention, had waited patiently.

"Darcy, what picture was that boy talking about?"

"The one you took after you started working out and got fine. Remember that?"

Chris thought about it for a minute and recalled the pictures she'd taken after a short relationship with a preacher back home that had charmed her to death, gotten into her panties, and then broken up with her—all within less than a month. Therapeutic for Chris, those pictures gave her a new lease on life.

"I gave you one of those pictures?"

"Actually, no. I took one. Anyway, he and his boys come over here almost every day and harass me nonstop about the girl in the picture. I never tell them shit because they're too damn nosy. When my phone rang tonight, they ran in here and tried to get it before I did. They just knew it was my man."

"Your man?"

"Bitch, you know better. You know damn well I ain't got no man."

"Aw!" Chris chuckled.

"I gotta put their asses outta my room," Darcy complained. "Hook me up! Hook me up, Darcy!" Annoyed, Chris' friend continued, "He and his friends are the most immature muthafuckas I've ever met."

Chris was flattered and, while her ego was doing flips, she had no interest in an underclassman. She had been fucking preachers, doctors, and lawyers…far too experienced for a schoolboy and way too bitchy for his kindness.

"What have you told him about me, Darcy?"

"Well, let's see. I mentioned the fact that you're smart as hell but a true bitch when you wanna be."

"To say the least."

"But I also told him that you're really a nice person who could use a nice gentleman friend. Nothing serious. Just a friend."

"And he said?"

"He still insisted on meeting you. He's got this image of his ideal woman being a redbone with an attitude. That's what he wants."

"I hate it when guys have this ready-made woman in their heads because if you do the niggah wrong, he'll hate you for life."

"True, but he's so damn desperate, girl. I don't think that he even cares. His mind isn't that mature yet. You gotta remember this, though."

"What?"

"He's so tight with his money that he squeaks, Chris."

"You know I could care less about a man and his money. That's why I try to keep my own. Besides, from what you've told me, he ain't got his hands on the right piece of ass yet. When he does, he'll set the dollars out quicker than he can make 'em."

"You two might hit it off, with you being so worldly and all. Let him hit that upperclassman ass a couple of times. He'll be running behind you like a newborn puppy."

Chris snickered. "I guess you've got a point. You have his number?"

Knowing full well she had no interest in a relationship, Chris was willing to take a chance. She'd made the decision to leave that other stuff alone.

"Yeah, I got it. Call him and leave a message. It'll fuck with him, that you called while he was out. He left here headed for campus to help one of his friends, and I know that's gonna take him a minute."

By two o'clock that morning, Darcy had informed Chris that Trey had his own car, lived in Maryland, was a communications major, and had a serious weakness for women. In spite of the fact that he was silly most of the time, Trey was really a nice guy. The only problem—he was a freshman and still had massive growing up to do. Oh, and it was determined that Trey was still a virgin.

The clock read four-seventeen a.m. when the telephone rang. Having been asleep only a couple of hours, Chris was groggy as hell.

"Hello." She sighed.

"May I speak to Chris?"

"Uh-huh. This is she."

"Hey, um, this is Trey. You talked to me over at Darcy's place?"

The refresher course wasn't necessary. Chris had an excellent memory and had just learned his life's history from Darcy. "Yeah, what's up? I see you got my message."

"Yes, I did. I'm sorry for calling you back so late or rather so early, but some friends of mine were having relationship problems and I was up on campus trying to help them out. I started to wait until…" Trey hesitated. "Well, I thought maybe I should wait until later today to call, but I really did want to talk to you."

Drifting in and out, Chris interjected, "I don't mean to cut you off, but I have got to get these last two hours of sleep in. I have to be at work at eight. Can you call me back later?"

Without hesitation, Trey said, "Sure, I can. What would be a good time?"

"I'm done with classes at three, and I have work study again until five."

"Will five-thirty be okay?"

"That's cool."

"Really, Chris, I'm sorry for disturbing you at this hour."

"No big deal, Trey. I'm glad you did."

Chris and Trey had their first date a couple of days later—with his two best friends, Bernard and Vance. All three were still schoolboy stupid. Everything was funny, everything had an inside joke and, for them, house music was their independence anthem. They felt that no date was complete without at least two of them in the car. Chris, much more seasoned than the trio, finally put her foot down with Trey and offered him some pussy. It was the only way she'd get to spend time alone with him and, believe it or not, she actually liked him.

Trey was the first guy that Chris had made wait for sex. It was almost two months before she allowed him to kiss her and almost three months before they finally found a place and some time to have a taste of each other's love. Chris got a hotel room, and they went at it for hours. Each time after that was either in his car, in Darcy's basement, or in the basement of the Woodley House—a house owned by the Methodist ministry on campus where Chris lived. Trey asked Chris to "school" him, and that she did. By the time Trey "graduated," his nose was so wide open you could drive a semi through it.

Thanks to his youth, Trey lacked the romance, the experience, and the substance that a woman like Chris needed. He never told her no, buying her everything that she asked for and then some. Little did he realize that he had created a problem that would inevitably facilitate their breakup. Trey was spoiled rotten by his parents and had no idea what it was like to have to be a real man. Cuddling with Chris and spending money on her were the only ways he knew how to give love. It didn't matter that they really had nothing in common, and Chris gave up on the hopes of the two of them having a romantic interlude accompanied by some classic Luther or Teena Marie. Trey just didn't have it in him. Chris loved this man, though, because he was nothing like her selfish and seemingly loveless father. Trey was the only man who'd paid attention to her, respected her, and wanted to be there for her. Despite the resentful attitudes of his circle of female friends, Chris came first—except when it came to his mother.

For three years, Chris and Trey created many special memories together. But the thorn in their otherwise idyllic, monogamous relationship was that Trey still lived at home with his parents. His mother cringed at the thought of her only son's involvement with just one woman—especially an older woman who kept him away from home so many nights. Chris, on the other hand, felt Trey was a man who needed to stop being a "momma's boy," so playing devil's advocate, she often encouraged him to spend the night with her and never wanted him out of her sight. Oh, and yes, Trey learned very quickly that Chris had a temper that wouldn't wait.

On the night Trey told Chris he was going out with some friends, she threw all of his clothes, bottles of cologne and other shit down a flight of stairs and called off the relationship, screaming, "I don't need a momma's boy, Trey! I need a real man! A man who knows his job is to be with me! Your friends act like they don't even know you've got a woman!"

Trey called his friends and canceled, but that wasn't enough for Chris. She still didn't let him back in the house and wouldn't even speak to him. Hoping she would forgive him, Trey kept his belongings in his trunk until she finally called…a week later. She never apologized, nor did she help him bring his things back into the house.

Another time Trey planned to visit some friends in New York and had no intention of taking Chris with him. The night before he was supposed to leave, she threw a tantrum at his parents' house, slinging his car keys into the bushes. In the pouring rain, the two of them checked every bush and shrub next to the house. After two hours, they finally found them and, as Trey walked away leaving Chris standing at the car, she hurled a 22-ounce bottle of Heineken at him. The bottle barely missed his head but, most importantly for him, he never turned back. The next day Chris came down with a terrible head cold and, unlike the other times, Trey did nothing to comfort her even when he returned from New York two days later.

The pivotal factor in the relationship was Chris' fear of being left alone because she was afraid of what she might do and with whom she might do it. She couldn't deny her attraction to women, but her unanticipated love for Trey would not allow her to surrender that part of her sexuality. Chris also feared that, like her father, Trey would ultimately lie to her about something. During her childhood, her father always lied—usually to be with another woman. As a child, Chris felt that it was cool that her daddy was a playa, sportin' one woman here and another woman there. But as she grew older and wiser, Chris realized there was more to that picture than met the eye. Her father always had more than one woman, just in case another pissed him off. Chris learned to never believe anything that her daddy told her. She despised him for the emotional abuse he'd inflicted on her mother and on so many other lives. Rather than be susceptible to such treatment, Chris exerted a dominating force over her relationship with Trey—insisting on knowing every step and every friend he made.

Graduation was an absolute godsend for Chris. She worked hard her final semester to make up two "incompletes" from the previous semester and immediately passed up all opportunities to attend grad school. Frustrated and burnt out from five years of papers, midterms, and study groups, Chris sometimes found it hard to believe that she'd finally made it. Freshman year Chris had become fascinated with her French instructor, Dr. Micaiah Monterrey. A California native and graduate of Stanford University, Dr. Monterrey's laid-back style of teaching was right up Chris' alley. On those mornings when she wasn't feeling the nine-ten start of class, Chris would slide into her seat around ten, always managing to avoid direct eye contact with her professor.

"Bonjour, Mademoiselle Desmereaux." Dr. Monterrey only communicated in French during class, and that was part of the reason why Chris came in so late in the very beginning. When midterms came around, Chris had mastered those common responses like "Je m'appelle Christian Desmereaux" and "C'est la vie." No matter what was asked of her those were the only responses she ever gave.

Her classmates and even Dr. Monterrey thought Chris' antics were hilarious, and it seemed impossible for her to pass the course with such a limited vocabulary. But no one laughed when Chris carried on a 30-minute conversation with the professor during finals. Each student was required to do at least fifteen minutes of dialogue as seventy-five percent of the final grade, and Chris had worked overtime at accomplishing just that. Her attendance sucked, as did her classroom participation, but she made up for it on her exams and quickly gained the respect of Dr. Monterrey.

Every semester of Chris' college career had included at least one or two of Dr. Monterrey's classes. Chris appreciated her leniency whenever she slacked off in class, for there were many mornings that Chris had come to class just to escape the confines of the dormitory. In addition to being attracted to Dr. Monterrey's teaching style, Chris actually did enjoy the beauty of the language and culture and didn't realize until the beginning of her last year in school that she'd accumulated enough credits in French course work to have a major in it. So when Chris walked across the stage in Greene Stadium that balmy Saturday afternoon in early May, she got two degrees: one in English Literature and the other in French. There were no academic honors for her, and Chris felt that her parents would be disappointed about that.

But when they realized that the family's first college graduate had doubled the return on their investment, they couldn't have been prouder. Ora, Carlos, and Iysha saw the two and a half hour outdoor ceremony as just a formality, and they fidgeted the entire time. It was almost as bad as sitting in church on Choir Day. And Trey, feeling as if he were the one most deserving of recognition for having to put up with Chris' bullshit, was sitting right there beside them.

Two months after graduation, Chris went back to Memphis for a visit and quickly realized that Memphis was no longer home. Before the summer ended, she was back in D.C. working at the Library of Congress. It wasn't her dream job, but it gave her some money and helped her keep that independence she'd worked so hard for.

4

The summer of '94 was a period of uncontrollable "feelings" for Chris, so she clung to Trey even tighter, wanting him all to herself and slamming the door on anyone daring to enter the world she had so meticulously crafted for just the two of them. Last-minute shopping sprees, student loan payments, and high long distance phone bills finally took their toll on Chris, and she was compelled to move in with Trey and his family. Chris resented this more than anything, but she had no choice. Darcy had gone to visit her family in Atlanta, and all of Chris' other girlfriends had moved back to their respective home-towns. Trey assumed that his parents wouldn't mind, so he never even bothered to ask their permission. He knew that Chris just needed enough time to save up money to get her own place.

It was late August when Chris began noticing these weird spontaneous cravings. While visiting Darcy upon her return from home, Chris hungered for King Dongs. She hadn't eaten them since her childhood, but she had to have them. Then she would kill for anything chocolate, devouring a bag of chocolate-covered peanuts in a single sitting. No need to worry. It was only PMS. Her wake-up call was her appetite for watermelon. Chris begged Trey to buy her a juicy, sweet melon but, because his family never bought or ate watermelons, Trey wasn't too anxious to bring one home.

"If I buy it, yo' ass is carryin' it!" he screamed at Chris while they were at the flea market. Like an African native carrying bushels of vegetables in the hot desert sun, Chris put the biggest watermelon she could find on her back and trotted to the car. Returning to the house, she sliced it once down the middle and got a fork.

"Damn, Chris, I didn't know that you were gonna make a meal of it," Trey said.

She ate one half at lunch and the other half less than three hours later.

Chris waited and waited on her period. Thinking she was only going through PMS, being pregnant was the furthest thing from her mind. But she also knew that the two of them had never been safe. After getting sick one summer from what felt like endless menstrual cramps, Chris was told that she had polycystic ovaries, which decreased her chances of getting pregnant by almost ninety percent. Green light! She and Trey went for it; their mutual desire for sex made it all the more gratifying. With an eighteen shoe size, Trey was packing the biggest dick that Chris had ever seen, and she often found herself reminiscing about the first time she'd touched it. Although she'd waited for sex with him, Chris had taken every opportunity to tease him about what he hadn't been able to get his hands on. He'd get so tickled about it that it'd make him rise to the occasion. Then one afternoon while they were riding in the car, the wind from the sunroof accidentally blew drops of a swiftly melting Popsicle on Trey's inner thigh. Chris took a napkin and started wiping up the mess while Trey kept one hand on the steering wheel and shifted gears with the other. Trey had been like a shaken-up can of soda waiting to explode, and with just one touch from Chris in that direction, he had erupted. Within seconds, Trey pulled over to a gas station, stretching his T-shirt down over his groin. Embarrassed, Chris apologized constantly after he got back in the car.

Sexually, they were definitely a perfect fit. Chris could be insatiable sometimes when it came to sex, and this time it mixed well with

Trey's inexperience. True, he lacked the sexual prowess of most men, but Chris didn't care. Her fascination with the size of his dick kept her mind off women and allowed her to focus on keeping potential home wreckers from her Howard man. A seemingly good man...with seemingly good manners...with seemingly good genes... with a definitely huge willy? Puh-leeze!

Chris rode Trey's ass morning, noon, and night and didn't give a damn about when her period came. Even though the doctor had said that there was a ninety-percent chance she'd never have a baby, Chris and Trey flirted heavily with that other ten percent. Sure, there were some false alarms, but she never even bothered to tell him about them. Those times were different from this one, though. Her mood had been horrible, she was always tired, and she couldn't stand to see Trey coming sometimes. It was so late this time that even Trey wondered what was up. Chris blamed its tardiness on stress and left it at that.

Finally, after two weeks of pacing, it came. Then, within twenty-four hours, it was gone. No spots, no streaks, no nothing. DAMN! That same night Chris and Trey went around the corner to Blockbuster to get a movie. Chris' mood had gone from being ecstatic to being absolutely miserable. Food didn't taste the same anymore, and nothing ever satisfied her. So she just chose not to eat and, in turn, that just made her feel worse.

"What's the matter with you tonight, Chris?" Trey asked as they stood at the checkout counter. "You haven't said much all evening."

Chris replied, "I'm fine. Just a little tired."

Paying the cashier, Trey took a closer look at Chris. "No, I've seen you tired before when you've gotten your period, and you've been nothing like this."

The cashier looked over at Chris, trying to see if she could possibly see whatever Trey saw.

Chris walked to the end of the counter to get the video. "I said, I'm fine."

Trey rushed ahead of Chris to get the door. "You insist on telling me nothing every time I ask."

"Look, let's not get into this out here. I don't want people all in my business."

"Bump them. Something's wrong."

Chris was helpless. She had no way out from this conversation, other than to start walking back to the house. Any other night she might have been able to do just that, but not tonight. "Trey, my period stopped."

"What do you mean, it stopped?"

"I mean, it started the day before yesterday, but now it's gone."

Reaching in his pocket for his keys, he took Chris' hand and walked across the parking lot to the car. Once they got in, he had to know more. "Is it gonna come back?"

Resting her head in her hands, she sighed. "I don't think so. I called Momma this afternoon, and she said that this had happened to her."

"And?"

"She later found out she was pregnant." Chris held her head down and wept. "I think I'm pregnant, Trey. That's got to be why I've been so out of it."

Unsure of what to say first, Trey ended up saying the wrong thing, and it wasn't comforting at all. "I thought you couldn't get pregnant. Isn't that what the doctor said?"

Chris saw where an obviously frustrated Trey was coming from. "You were sitting right there when he told me that there was only a ninety-percent chance of that, and you also heard him say not to take any chances with it."

"Right, and I also remember you telling him that you didn't want to take the pill. You shouldn't have done that."

"What! The pill is what caused the problem in the first place! I haven't seen you run your ass to the drugstore for raincoats. 'Naw, baby, don't worry about it,' you always say. 'Let me keep it in just one more minute,' you said. Well, Trey, it didn't take but a minute, and I can't believe you're acting this way."

Realizing that neither of them was ready for a long drawn out argument, Trey gradually calmed down. "Tell you what. Let's find out for sure tomorrow. There's no need to get all worked up about it now. There may be something else going on."

"Thank you. I just can't take an argument tonight. I'll make an appointment at one of those birthright centers. It's quick and discreet."

"Okay, we'll go first thing in the morning."

▲

The Right to Life Center was able to take Chris right away. After she took the pregnancy test, she and Trey were asked to watch a film about abortion. It was obvious that the counselors were pro-choice advocates because every five minutes somebody wanted to know if Chris and Trey would consider adoption if they didn't want to go through with the pregnancy. At that point Trey, overwhelmed with the possibility of becoming a parent long before he was ready, calmly asked to be left alone until the results had come back.

Approximately ten minutes after taking Chris' urine to the back room, the counselor emerged, clutching a black binder. Trey took a break from pacing and sat down next to an obviously nervous Chris. Squeezing her hand, he consoled her. "It's going to be all right, baby."

Chris just nodded her head and awaited the counselor's findings.

Mrs. Gomez, a twenty-year veteran in this business, had often found herself in awkward situations such as this one. She took a seat across from Chris and opened the binder. "I have a listing of OB-GYNs and clinics in the area. I..."

Without hearing another word, Trey immediately felt that he had to celebrate and didn't conceal his elation. "See, Chris, she's going to help you find out what's wrong. I told you it was nothing to be worried about!"

Puzzled by Trey's reaction, Mrs. Gomez quickly interjected, "Baby, your girlfriend is about seven weeks pregnant. That's what's wrong with her."

"She's pregnant?"

"Yes, she is. I figured that she might be once I heard some of her symptoms. I need to first ask you two if you have considered your options."

"What options?"

"Well, if you decide not to keep the baby for whatever reason, we can help you. There's the matter of adoption and such, and there's also abortion."

A tearful Chris spoke for the first time since hearing the news. "None of those are options. I'm keeping the baby." Chris had made the decision not long after she had first suspected that she might be pregnant. She had a job and a college education, so she figured she could handle it even if she had to do it alone. "Oh, and Trey?"

Clearing his throat, a saddened Trey snapped, "What?"

"It's not up for discussion. With or without you, I'm doing this."

As a trained family counselor, Mrs. Gomez's heart went out to both of them, for she'd seen situations like theirs far more times than she'd ever imagined. The mother wanted it, but the father didn't. Chris, consumed by the radiance of an expectant mother, was distracted by the outward disappointment of her boyfriend of almost four years. Trey was heartbroken, and the tears he'd withheld began to stream freely down through his freshly manicured beard.

Mrs. Gomez always kept a box of Kleenex on her desk, and during her twenty years at the center, it never failed that she'd run out of tissues by the end of the day. In this session alone, Chris and Trey had used over half the box—eventually taking those that remained in the box out the door with them. For the parents-to-be, it was a long ride home.

Finding out that she was pregnant gave Chris a dismal look into the best and worst of the fragile world that she'd created for Trey and herself. The best of that world was believing that Trey was going to marry her, now that she was pregnant with his child. She knew it was inevitable because his upbringing commanded it. Although they had conflict, just as most couples do, their relationship was stable, and because her own upbringing reflected what life was like when a real father wasn't around, Chris was ecstatic. Chris had a man with seemingly good genes and morals. He respected and loved her deeply, and Chris knew that he'd never turn his back on her or their child. They both had an education from Howard and had the potential for promising careers. Once the baby was born, the three of them would attend Howard homecoming games, proudly seated among other distinguished alumni wearing Howard sweatshirts and other school paraphernalia. And when that baby graduated from HU, the three of them would attend all alumni festivities, hoping to create another generation of Howardites.

Trey had a huge willy and, with a little more help, he'd be a man about his business in the bedroom. Most importantly, she'd be able to show her family what the world could have waiting for you if you'd just step outside the county line. All of that was what Chris considered to be the best of her world, but it was overshadowed by the worst of her world that seemed to mimic reality. Soon after discovering she was pregnant, Chris began to see how cruel a mother could be when trying to protect her son.

▲

Mr. and Mrs. Marvin Withers' first child was stillborn. The younger Mrs. Withers blamed the baby's death on the emotional turmoil created by the elder Mrs. Withers, Marvin's mother. The elder Mrs. Withers detested her son's choice in women. The very first girl he dated made him do some stupid shit. He stayed out all hours of the night. He never had any money to contribute to the household, and he stayed on the telephone all the time. When Marvin brought his girl home to meet his family, everyone, except his mother, was cordial. Mrs. Withers barely mumbled a word to Teresa when she passed through the family room and then, while gathering her personal belongings along the way, she retired to her bedroom whenever Teresa visited thereafter. It was Marvin's father who always threw out the welcome mat, and it was also his father who gave the family's blessings when Marvin and Teresa got married.

During the first months of their marriage, Mrs. Withers never went to her son's home nor did she ever call. Teresa's parents, however, loved their new son-in-law to death. He had manners and was always respectful whenever he visited. Mr. Fulton, Teresa's father, was a retired family practitioner and had given his wife and only child the best of everything. Mrs. Fulton never had to work and, while at home all day, she taught her daughter how to be a lady and how to earn the respect of her man by staying out of his affairs. She did not want to see her in the same predicament as herself, a stay-at-home mother with only a high school education unable to compete with her husband's female colleagues who were physicians and nurses. At holiday parties Mrs. Fulton made sure that the house was immaculately decorated and that everything, down to the entertainment, was perfect. While the others discussed "shop" and office politics, their hostess simply cleared the dishes and kept the hot coffee coming. The Fultons welcomed everyone into their home; no matter what their social class.

One night after leaving Marvin's parents' house, Teresa burst into tears.

"What's wrong, honey?" he asked.

Looking at her husband, she replied, "Why doesn't your mother like me? I haven't done anything to her."

"I don't know, Teresa. She's never said anything to me about it."

"I get tired of sitting in the car whenever we go over there. She hasn't spoken a word to me since you first introduced us. We've been married for almost a year and, even when we told her that the baby died, she had nothing to say."

Marvin did know why his mother kept her jaws so tight when it came to Teresa. He was the only son she had left. His older brother, Derric, had committed suicide over his very first girlfriend, Lisa. Knowing that Derric was head-over-heels in love with her, Lisa played games with him about being pregnant and about dating other guys. One afternoon, as he was passing by her apartment building, Derric spotted the car that he had helped Lisa buy the day before. The windows were foggy, and the radio speakers were thumping. He peeped through the cracked window and saw Lisa's naked ass perched on the groin of another man. Derric called Lisa's name and, as soon as she showed her face, he intentionally stepped into the path of oncoming traffic. From that point on, Marvin's mother had held contempt for any other woman that entered her family.

Mrs. Withers made it clear that no girls were to come to her home while her son was in high school. So, while Marvin courted Teresa, he spent lots of time at school and at a nearby soda shop. The day after he graduated, Marvin brought his bride-to-be home and introduced her to the family. When he returned from taking Teresa home, Mrs. Withers was still awake, waiting for him in the dark.

"You been lying to me, Marvin?"

"Ma'am?" he asked, closing the door.

His mother's voice had that "you-know-you've-fucked-up" tone. "You've been seeing that girl behind my back, haven't you?"

Marvin wasn't really sure what he was supposed to say. A "yes" would mean a smack upside the head with whatever was nearby. A "no" meant that he was still afraid of his mother and no matter what he proclaimed his feelings to be for Teresa, they meant nothing in front of her. He was eighteen, though, and it was time for something to give.

"Mom, look, ever since Derric died, I've lived under your roof, under your rules. I come home before the sun goes down, and I faithfully do every chore on your list of one hundred and one things for me to do. It's time for me to have a life."

"Don't you see that they're all just useless tramps? Those girls don't know anything about love."

"What makes you such an expert? You've had me too afraid to bring girls here to the house. I have to sneak them in and out of here hoping that you don't catch me. Now, I'm tired of sneaking."

Marvin stepped toward the door as his mother cut her eyes at him. She was notorious for throwing anything when she was angry.

"Mom, you want to know why I love Teresa so much?"

"Not really. I don't care why you do."

"Well, I'm going to tell you anyway." He moved toward the sofa and sat next to his mother, taking her hand. Marvin felt an energy around his mother and, in it, he felt his brother's spirit. "I love her, Mom, because she reminds me of what you used to be before Derric died."

Tears streamed down Mrs. Withers' face. She reached for her cup of tea and took a sip. Glancing at a picture of Derric, she knew in her heart that she blamed every woman in the world, including herself, for her son's demise. That was something she would never admit to anyone. Without another word, she got up and again retired to her bedroom.

When Marvin and Teresa got home that night, Marvin shared his mother's grief with his wife, explaining to her that his mother's anger was not her fault. The love they made created a child, and Trey Thurman Withers was born nine months later. Because she'd died in her sleep two weeks before he was born, Trey—to his benefit and to his mother's satisfaction— never knew his grandmother, Mrs. Irma Withers. So it was natural that Trey loved women and was not ashamed to say it. He loved them with school boyish-like tendencies, giggling all the time and saying stupid shit for attention. His mother gave him everything and had him in everything...the Boy Scouts, Jack and Jill. Before he was fifteen, he had toured Europe, and a year later he was given his first car.

The girls in his neighborhood were not only his friends but were his mother's first choices when it came to whom her son dated. They were from good families, and she knew their parents. None were from broken homes, and all had intentions of attending college. Full of common courtesy and respect, each entered her home knowing their place and keeping it. Trey, giddy and always unsuspecting, could never tell when his mother's and a female friend's personalities clashed. Thus, he was blind as a bat when the problems started between Chris and his mother.

▲

Chris was at a birthday party for Trey's cousin when she and Mrs. Withers were first introduced. During the entire afternoon, their conversation was casual but tense. Teresa could immediately tell that Chris was more mature than her son and that maybe, just maybe, he was out of her league.

"So what year in school are you, honey?" she'd asked.

Trey had told her once before that she was a senior, but she wanted to hear it straight from the horse's mouth.

"I'm a senior but, from the looks of things, I might need another year."

"Oh," Teresa replied. Her son was only a baby compared to her. "Have you made any post graduate plans?"

She was hoping that Chris would say that she would be leaving the country or something. Trey didn't need this one.

"Not really. I'll probably take a little break and go back to school." Chris didn't have a clue as to what was going through Teresa's mind. "In the meantime, I hope to settle down."

What? Teresa thought. Oh, no, my son isn't even going down this road with you! I'll see to that.

While keeping the phoniest smile that Chris had ever seen, she said, "Well, it was nice meeting you, Chris. I hope to see more of you. You should really come out to the house soon."

Little did she know, Chris and Trey had been going to her house pretty regularly in the afternoons for a quickie.

To his mother's disappointment, Trey brought Chris to the house almost every day. Whenever Teresa saw Trey, her smile radiated the room. But within seconds, Chris would appear in the doorway, and that radiant smile would turn into a frown of "Damn, there that bitch is again!"

Trey's mother immediately saw that her son and his new girlfriend were inseparable. When Trey started taking loads of clothes over to Chris' apartment, Teresa just ground her teeth, fearing she'd lose her son if she openly objected.

His evenings became long nights, and days would pass before he would go home. As quiet as it was kept, it was no real surprise when Chris became pregnant. Calm and seemingly in charge of his feelings, Trey shit bricks about the baby. He whined to all his female friends and cried on the shoulders of his boys. At first, the thought was beautiful but when the reality of having to tell his mother hit home, the idea of being a daddy wasn't so pretty after all.

The very morning of the day Trey had planned to tell his mother about the baby, Chris' morning sickness was in full effect. From that morning on, that sickness became a ritual and usually lasted most of the day. The excuses for it were running out, and with the nausea and vomiting lasting almost all day, it was becoming increasingly difficult to hide. Telling his mother was not going to be easy. Trey figured the best way to do it was out in the open where she couldn't react. So, he called her at work and asked her to meet him for lunch. Appreciative of her son's unusual but kind gesture, Mrs. Withers knew something was up, but she still obliged and met him in Georgetown at Houston's.

While Mrs. Withers rode in the back of the cab, she—through that natural, maternal instinct—figured out what Trey wanted. As much as that revelation hurt, she was determined to let him be a man by giving him his moment. Trey was already seated when his mother arrived. He had rehearsed his speech over and over. By the end of the coming hour, maybe, just maybe, a full-grown man would emerge.

"So what's this all about? My son wanting to have lunch with me." Mrs. Withers smiled as she leaned in to kiss him.

Trey knew his mother all too well and detected that she was suspicious. "Um, I just wanted to spend some time with you."

Bullshit! Taking off her jacket, Mrs. Withers asked, "Are you sure about that?"

"Yeah, that's all," he said, taking a sip of water. "Order whatever you want. It's on me."

"Trey, can you afford to do this? I can pay for my own food."

"Don't worry about it, Mom. I've got it."

Mrs. Withers placed her order when the waitress came and then just jumped right into it. "You brought me here to tell me that Chris is pregnant, didn't you?"

Knowing that his mother was right—as she usually was—Trey nodded his head and took another sip of water. "Um, how'd you know?"

"First, I'm your mother, and I know everything. Second, you haven't been yourself lately, and finally, I heard her in the bathroom this morning just like I did yesterday and the day before that. What's she planning to do?"

"She wants to have it."

"Well, I figured that. Giving consideration to the fact that she's living with us—which means her money isn't right—and taking into account that you're still a baby—my baby at that—I think she needs to have an abortion. That's all there is to it."

Her well-done steak and baked potato arrived at the table, and she slid the plate next to her untouched garden salad. "You should've been bringing yourself home all those nights. The two of you spend entirely too much time together. She controls your every move, and you're too young for all that."

"Mom..."

"Let me finish," she continued. "I was the first woman that your father ever dated, and I have regretted that for years."

Trey was confused. "I don't understand."

Clearing her throat, she explained her comment. "I can tell that he often wonders what other women are like. I see him looking from time to time, and I can't say anything because I know that he's just being a man." Teresa grabbed her son by the arm and asked, "I know you think about other women, don't you?"

Trey blushed. "Yeah, Mom, I do, but I still love Chris. She looks at other men, and it doesn't bother me because I know that she loves me. She says that she's going to do this, with or without me."

Teresa suddenly had flashbacks of her husband's mother. "Do you want me to talk to her?"

That would be like feeding Chris to the lions and would further complicate things, Trey thought. Trey really did love Chris, but he simply wasn't ready for a baby. Hearing the truth from another woman might be easier for Chris to handle.

"Look, you can try, but I doubt if it does much good. And if you can, please be nice. She hasn't been feeling too well."

"Honey, that's part of being pregnant. I'll talk to her when I get home."

Another woman's advice might have been helpful for Chris, just as long as that woman was not Mrs. Withers. Approaching Chris with a check for three-hundred dollars was probably not the best way to tell Chris that she needed to have an abortion. She just burst into the bedroom and started in on Chris.

"That boy is not ready to be somebody's daddy, and I think you know that. So, here."

Chris glanced at the check and shook her head in disbelief. "Mrs. Withers," Chris said calmly, "Trey is not the only issue here. I believe you know that and just aren't willing to accept it. I realize he's young, and I've considered the consequences of it. When it comes down to it, this is my decision, and I wish you'd respect it. I don't want your money."

Chris turned to a pile of clothes that she'd been gathering from the floor and started folding them. Her chest throbbed fiercely, and her head was spinning. This conversation was inevitable; so she figured that she might as well get it over with and took a seat on the edge of the bed.

"Chris, don't you realize how gullible he is? That boy can't find his way out of a paper bag—let alone find his way to becoming a father to this baby."

"I hate to be rude, but don't you think that you've had something to do with that? Trey can't please me for trying to please you. When I need him to be with me, he wants to be here with you. You baby him. You still buy his clothes and cook all of his meals. Right now, he's not any good to any other woman but you."

Furious, Mrs. Withers stepped over Trey and Chris' belongings that had been strewn about the cramped bedroom and slammed the door.

"You're trying to trap my son," she said as her voice quivered and her eyes glistened with tears. "He's a good man, and..."

"That's right. He is a good man, and you should be proud of him. But this good man—your son, your baby—made a baby. We're both at fault for being careless, and I'm not going to let what I consider to be my blessing suffer because of that. Now, I know he's trying to graduate, and he doesn't need this burden. In addition to this never-ending attitude that I get from you, I struggle with trying to be considerate of Trey's need to focus on getting through his last year of school. So don't you ever accuse me of trapping him. All I have left to say is that you'd better hope that I don't have a girl because if I do, it'll just give you one more woman to compete with."

"You're ruining him. I hope you know that."

"I'm ruining him no more than you already have, Mrs. Withers."

Chris brushed past Trey's mother and left the house. Being alone with people that she had come to trust as her own family, Chris had no outlet, no refuge. She soon began to see that even Trey had some resentment toward her for causing his mother's disappointment in him. After weeks of silence, Trey's father finally spoke up and told them that they would probably end up on welfare. Nevertheless, Chris, at this point in her life where all of her friends had careers and real lives, was lonely and needed someone there so that Trey might have his freedom to enjoy his life and his final year at Howard. It was either a woman or a baby and, given the circumstances, a baby was the most sensible answer.

By late October, Chris had received so much animosity from Trey's mother that she thought it best to quit her job and return to Memphis. In an effort to further convince Chris that she needed to return home, Ora had promised to help pay her bills. All of the money in her savings account was spent on buying a last-minute ticket home. Her morning sickness had begun to last all day, and she was tremendously stressed out. The night before she left, Chris tried to show Trey's mother an ultrasound picture of the baby that had been taken earlier in the day.

"Mrs. Withers, look at what we have," she said, pulling the picture from a brown envelope. Chris almost had to force the picture into her hands.

"What's this?" questioned Mrs. Withers as she approached Chris to give her a hug good-bye. Beginning her well-rehearsed farewell, she said, "I won't be up when you get ready to leave in the morning, so…" She paused, looking at the paper. "What's this?"

"It's the baby," Trey responded. "Can't you…"

"Oh," she replied, handing the picture back to Chris. "Anyway, I just came down to wish you well, and to tell you to be careful."

"Thank you," Chris replied. "And thank you for letting me stay here."

"No problem." She grinned as she headed down the hallway.

The once proud mother-to-be was pitiful after that. She had to fight back tears, for it was not the first time that Mrs. Withers had ignored the fact that Chris was carrying her grandchild. Mrs. Withers carried on casual conversation with Chris about almost everything and, not once, did she ever inquire about the baby. It was Chris' first child. She was exploding with joy and had so many questions for her child's grandmother—the only adult she had access to and could confide in. But she soon realized that nothing could compete with the love that a mother has for her son and vice-versa. The next morning, as the plane took off from Washington National Airport, Chris closed her eyes and cried for three reasons. For one, she was leaving behind her baby's father. In her heart Chris felt that they would never be a family because Trey wasn't ready to grow up. He had asked Chris to let him grow at his own pace—a pace that had no measure. Two, Trey's family didn't want this child. Melanie, Trey's sister, was the only person that seemed to care that Chris was giving birth to her first niece or nephew. Every morning before leaving for work, she asked Chris if there was anything she needed. Relieved that she was finally able to return Trey to his mother, Chris felt she could concentrate on a healthy, stress-free pregnancy. And three, at the age of 24, even though she had finally earned those precious Howard University degrees, Chris realized that she was no more than what she was when she had come to D.C. six years before. Haunted by thoughts of welfare, no man, no job, and a fucked up life, Chris knew that she had only regressed.

5

Memphis wasn't a place known for making a lot of changes, and its citizens were just the same. You could still find a good selection of curl activator in the health and beauty section of any department store; some of the older radio stations still had the same DJs from twenty years before—those stations were still ranked first in the ratings—and the same man that had sold Chris' mother the best tamales some ten years earlier was still on the same corner. The only thing that had changed was that he had a bigger and better tamale cart. So Chris knew that she could count on everything at home still being the same. The love of family was there, but at what sacrifice, she didn't know. When her plane touched down, she wondered what the city held for her because no matter how hard she'd tried to stay away, she was always pulled back to the area for one reason or another. She just kept praying for everything to be stable enough for her to have a healthy pregnancy, so that she could return to the place she now called home. All things considered, however, a year's sentence in Memphis might not be so bad.

No one was at the gate when Chris emerged from the jetway, but she was used to that. Nobody in her family was ever on time. As she walked through the terminal, the urge to pee hit with a vengeance, and she headed for the bathroom. She'd held it the entire trip and, after a can of cranberry juice, Ora would just have to wait.

"There my baby is!" Ora squealed as she spotted Chris adjusting her clothes as she left the ladies' room. "Look at you!"

Chris had a little bulge on top of the big bulge in her stomach. She'd put on quite a bit of weight before she got pregnant and wasn't the least bit ashamed.

"Hey, Momma!" she exclaimed, extending her arms toward her mother. "It's so good to see you."

Chris, although she'd never tell her, missed her mother tremendously. Already spoiled rotten, Chris believed that she'd made the right decision by returning home. Sure, she'd miss Trey, but he'd promised to visit for Christmas.

"Let's go get your bags. Pete's outside waiting in the loading zone. You hungry?"

"Yes, I am. Can you cook me some breakfast please, Momma? Oh-ma God, I'm about to starve!"

It was the first time that there was no morning sickness, no flatulence, no nausea. Chris was home.

Without any health insurance or money, Chris went directly to the Memphis Department of Human Services. Because coverage under COBRA would not have extended to Tennessee, Chris was stuck. Mr. Withers' premonition about welfare was hitting home, and the only thing on Chris' mind was that she was determined not to take or need the government's money, if she didn't have to.

"Chris Desmereaux!" a husky voice called from the middle of a room filled with indigent Black folks who didn't have jobs, health insurance or food on the table. This status qualified them for a wealth of opportunities, free opportunities. The spacious room used to be a discount department store and was large enough to hold over a thousand people all at once. Every DHS office was housed in the same type of space. "Chris Desmereaux!" the voice called again. "D-E-S-M-E..."

Chris assumed she was supposed to respond, "Here I am." That was the only way she'd be recognized, but Chris' pride wouldn't let her do that. She stepped over a woman and her five children and was relieved that, after three hours of waiting and six trips to the nastiest rest room she'd ever seen, she was finally being called. It seemed that with every passing hour at least seventy-five people walked through the door, not to mention the ones standing outside just hangin' out to see what was going on at the food stamp office. As Chris approached the tall man who bore a striking resemblance to her mother's boyfriend, she couldn't help but notice the reason why she could barely hear her name. Each caseworker was coming to the same spot in the huge room and calling a client's name.

"Shaneka James!!!!!!!!!!!!!" a woman yelled.

"Donte Spencer!!!!!!!!!!!!!" another woman screamed.

"Metissa Jones!!!!!!!!!!!!!" a man roared.

And then the funniest thing, a wimpy, little White man—one of very few—was calmly whispering, "Geraldine Smith."

All of this at the same time. All of this in the same spot. All of this in one room.

Chris walked up to the man that had called her name and said simply, "I'm Chris."

As she passed the tiny cubicles, Chris could hear the various conversations taking place. One client was explaining how she'd lost her food stamps and needed to feed her babies. Chris had just seen her out front talking about how she'd sold her stamps to pay her car note. Another client was pissed because her welfare check hadn't come and wanted to know who the supervisor was. Yet, in another cubicle, a man was explaining how he couldn't find a job and that getting up before ten in the morning was way too early for him. His caseworker was arguing with him because he'd seen him in the food stamp line at 7 a.m. There seemed to be endless excuses for complacency. What was she doing here?

Her caseworker, Mr. Dandridge, seemed nice. Still sportin' his afro and curl, he was an educated man, with his degree from LeMoyne-Owen College hanging from a nail in the wall of his cubicle. "How do you say your name?" He chuckled.

"First or last?" Chris responded.

"Both." He laughed. "It's pretty, if I could pronounce it."

"Well, the first is just like it looks. I know you've seen it before."

"Like the religious stuff, right?"

"Uh-huh. But Chris is just fine."

"And the last? Is it French or something?"

"Yes." She smiled. "My dad's part Creole. Don't worry about trying to pronounce it. Just as long as you spell it right. Okay?"

"All right, then, Chris. What can we do for you?"

"Well, I'm pregnant, and I don't have any health insurance."

"Okay. First, let me give you some papers to fill out. You married?"

"No," Chris answered. She started completing the papers.

"Well, here are your options. The State will provide you with health insurance. You're free to go to any doctor that accepts Medicaid. They'll handle everything else, and you only see us again to be re-certified. We have to keep a file on you, and you'll be assigned a caseworker. By the way, you're in the wrong office. You have to go out on Jackson Avenue to that office."

"Is it like this one?"

"Actually, it's worse." He smiled. He glanced over her application and noticed that she refused an AFDC check. "You don't want a check? That's what they always come here for."

He stopped and looked at Chris, who had become very uneasy and hungry.

"I don't want a check, and I'm not them," she said, pointing toward the waiting area. "I just need the health insurance."

Mr. Dandridge became curious. "Are you from here originally? You don't have an accent," he said, looking over the application.

"I was born here, but I went to college in D.C."

"I was just wondering because you seem so intelligent. I mean, you seem to have some sense of pride, and you aren't trying to run some game on me. Don't see that much around here."

"I came back here to have my baby. My boyfriend is still in school at Howard."

"Howard University?" he questioned. "You went there, too?"

"Yes, I graduated last year." She hiccupped. Chris was starving. "I don't mean any harm, but are we almost done?"

"Yeah, I hear your stomach growling." He laughed. "Seriously, though, you're entitled to a check every month. It's only about ninety-five dollars."

"What's it for?"

"Just some extra money for you and the baby. Nothing other than that. You should also look into getting WIC."

"What?"

He handed her a pamphlet. "This will explain everything. If you have any questions, just call me and I'll help as best I can."

"Thanks." Chris glanced over the freebies and still insisted on asking one last question. Mr. Withers' comment about welfare was still in the back of her mind. "Do I have to take the check?"

"If it makes you feel better, it's not AFDC. There's another technical name for it. Just keep them—just in case."

"Okay. Thank you again." She turned around and headed toward the main aisle.

"Oh, and Chris?" he added. "The State is always hiring. Maybe after the baby comes, you can take the state employment test. It'll qualify you for more than just one job. I have an extra application in my desk."

Mr. Dandridge knew that Chris was a strong African-American woman who was simply having a bad time and failed to see it as only being temporary. Hadn't anyone ever told her that these things happen to the best of us? She was very articulate, with the absence of a Southern drawl. She had been refined—in a subtle way—during her years in Washington. He fiddled a minute and finally pulled out a stack of papers.

"Here it is. You'll be able to pass the test with no problem."

This caught Chris completely by surprise, but she was grateful for the help. Taking the application, she smiled at the caseworker and made her way to the front door. Chris was determined that she'd never tell Trey that she was getting that check. The last thing she wanted was to give any credence to Mr. Withers' comment.

Once she met her new caseworker, she never mentioned Trey's name and was persistent about not knowing where he was. Every re-certification meeting was the same. It was explained that if the baby's father surfaced, the State would pursue him for reimbursement and would also collect child support from him. Trey wasn't a deadbeat dad, so there was no need to tell more than what was asked. Besides, he was sending Chris an allowance on his own.

Emotionally, pregnancy was not all that Chris had hoped it would be. Her mother was so caught up in keeping up with Pete that she rarely had any time to bond with Chris. Ora made sure that Chris made it to her doctor's appointments on time and even made arrangements for a private phone line to be put in Chris' room. Trey called every night to make sure that everything was going okay, but Chris soon began to notice that his tone and manner weren't what they used to be. He lacked interest in her and seemed to reluctantly have an obligated interest in the baby. For Christmas, he visited Chris and finally saw a better ultrasound of what turned out to be his daughter. Chris, who had deeply wanted a son, was disappointed but relished the idea that she'd given Trey another woman to worship. She was still, however, waiting on an engagement ring. The holiday season came and went with no mention of a ring or marriage.

Chelsea Marie Desmereaux was born in March of 1995 and

brought much warmth to her mother's heart. Chris kept so busy with motherhood that there was no time for thoughts of being alone. She had taken the government checks and saved them up to buy a ticket to D.C. for Trey's graduation that May. When Trey first laid eyes on his daughter, tears filled his eyes, and when he reached for her, he cradled her with warmth and affection. Chris and Chelsea stayed with Darcy while in D.C. because Chris refused to stay at Trey's house…with that woman. Trey had bought baby wipes, diapers, a stroller, and a ton of clothes, hoping that Chris would change her mind, but she didn't. Mrs. Withers didn't call even once after Chelsea was born, nor did she ever initiate conversation when Chris called for Trey. By this time, Chris had found her conduct reprehensible, but who cared what Chris thought? Trey never said anything about it and, to keep the drama down, neither did Chris.

Darcy, however, didn't hold her tongue. "Trey, you and I are friends, right?" she asked him one night while he was trying to change Chelsea's diaper. Chris had gone out to get something to eat.

Trey, tussling with the tape on the diaper, had already gone through three. "How the hell is this shit supposed to work!" he screamed, balling up yet another Pamper.

Darcy didn't want to laugh at him because poor Trey probably would have burst into tears. "Let me help you. In case you haven't noticed, these things aren't cheap. Chris will have a fit when she sees that you've already thrown away four of them." She pulled out another diaper and explained the art of changing a baby's diaper to him, realizing that he just didn't understand what he was doing. "Trey, have you talked with Chris?"

"About what?" he asked, taking the baby in his arms.

"This whole thing with your mother."

"Oh, that. They'll both be all right and get over it before you know it."

"I don't think so. Trey, even though it doesn't seem like it, this is killing Chris. She hasn't done anything wrong, but she's getting flack like she did. I mean, she left your ass here so that you could get your degree like we got ours."

"Wouldn't you have done the same thing?"

"Hell, no. I would've stayed up here and made your ass be responsible. She shouldn't have had to go through this alone."

"She wasn't by herself, Darcy. She had her family. Dang!"

"Whether you realize it or not, that was your responsibility. You should've never let her leave."

"Well..." He smirked. "It's too late to even be bothered with that. The baby's here now."

"She sure is, and what part do you intend to play in her life?"

"Darcy, I don't know. I haven't thought much about it."

"Are you planning to marry Chris?"

"I'm going to give her a ring before she leaves. I picked it out last weekend. And you better not tell her! You know how you two gossip."

"I won't say anything, but you still haven't said anything about your mom. I think you need to talk to her about how she's been treating Chris."

"I will." Trey wasn't listening to Darcy. He never listened to anyone who tried to advise him about anything concerning his mother. Completely disregarding everything they'd talked about, Trey blurted, "Have you ever seen Chris breast-feeding?"

Darcy then realized how silly Trey truly was. "No, I haven't. She only breast-feeds her at night when she's too tired to get up and make a bottle."

"That shit blew my mind the first time I saw her whip that thing out! She did it while I was trying to get a bottle ready for Chelsea."

"Trey?" Darcy saw that he'd changed the subject on his own and would find any additional conversation on the subject useless.

"What?"

"Never mind."

The first time that Mrs. Withers saw Chelsea she didn't even want to hold her. She simply said, "Oh, she's cute," and turned away. Chris was determined that she wasn't going to get upset. What took the cake, however, was the incident at Trey's post-graduation party.

Mrs. Withers' best friend, Nora, walked in and saw Mr. Withers holding the baby. Chris was making bottles, and Trey was putting together a swing. "Whose baby is this?" Nora squealed. "She sure is a pretty lil' thang." No one said a word.

For almost five minutes, there was complete silence. Mrs. Withers kept cooking dinner, Mr. Withers kept holding Chelsea, and Trey kept working on the swing. Just as Chris was about to speak up, Mrs. Withers muttered quickly, "That's Trey's baby, honey," as if it were some embarrassment for her. She never looked up from her cooking, and no one else said a word.

"Well, congratulations...I guess." It was obvious Nora was hurt that her best friend had kept this secret from her. She picked up a drink and headed out the patio door.

That did it for Chris. During the entire trip, she and her daughter remained at Darcy's—despite Trey's objections.

Chris' one-week visit turned into a month of reckoning. One night while she and the baby were at Trey's, Trey got up and took the baby into his mother's room. "Can you watch her for me?" he asked, placing Chelsea's diaper bag and bottle on the bed. "I need to take Chris out for a while so she can get some air."

"Well, I can't right now. I..."

"Okay, I just gave her a bath and here's her bottle. It'll probably be late when we get back." He never gave his mother a chance to say another word.

One thing Chris knew for certain was that Trey was not a romantic. Bless his heart, he tried, but it never seemed to be enough.

"Where's the baby?" Chris inquired. "I know you didn't leave her with your mother?"

"Yes, I did. It'll give them a chance to get to know each other. Besides, I want to spend some time with you."

Trey got his keys and told Chris to come with him.

The ride into D.C. took about twenty minutes and during that time, Trey, fearing that he might spoil his surprise, spoke very little to Chris. Standing a little over six feet tall, Trey towered above Chris' five-foot-six frame. Over the years, he had seemed to shed his youthful look and now took great care in making sure that he was perfectly groomed whenever he left the house. Chris took credit for that because she never hesitated to tell him when his breath smelled bad or when he had that not-so-fresh odor about him. When they'd first met, his table manners had been atrocious, and Chris called him out one night in front of his friends while they'd sat there listening to him smack his lips together while eating. Later, she admitted that she was wrong for doing that, but it irritated her to watch them let him eat that way. It was several months before she agreed to go out to dinner with him again.

Chris had also been responsible for tightening up Trey's wardrobe. She bought him his first tailored suit, complete with matching handkerchief and tie. Still, she knew that no matter how much she tried to mold him, Trey was still young and had massive growing to do. Trey appreciated all of her help but could never understand why Chris went through all that trouble. All she'd ever say is, "Why would I want somebody that nobody else would want?" So with that, Trey—with his smooth brown skin, beautiful smile, warm personality, buff chest, and now a Howard degree—was ready to ask Chris to be his wife.

He stopped the car on Sixth Street, right in front of Douglass Hall. Chris looked around at the dark HU campus and immediately asked why they were there.

"You know what this place is?" Trey smiled.

"Well, yes, I do. Why are we here?"

"This is the place where I actually first saw you."

"What?"

"That day I was supposed to call you I first saw you right here crossing the street. You were hurrying toward the "A" building. By the time I got my window down, you had already gone in. I had gazed at your picture so many times that there was no mistaking who you were."

Chris guessed that Trey had finally found a little romance and was getting ready to pop the question. "Why have you never said anything about that?"

"That was my private moment about you—the one that I'll never forget. I was saving it for something special, and tonight is something special." Trey reached under his seat and pulled out a little black velvet box and proceeded to open it. "Chris, will you marry me?"

Reaching for the interior light to help her see, Chris took one look at the quarter of a carat solitaire and immediately said, "Yes."

Her response, however, lacked the excitement that Trey had anticipated. "I know the diamond is small. When I get some more money..."

Taking her index finger and gently placing it over Trey's lips, Chris pulled him to her and assured him that what she had was fine. As she hugged him and studied her ring, she found comfort in knowing that the waiting was finally over.

The next day Chris and Darcy took Chelsea to the zoo. They knew that the baby would never remember being there, but it gave them a chance to get out of the house and to also have a girlfriend-to-girlfriend talk about the engagement.

"So are you gonna tell me, or do I have to pull it out of you?" Darcy asked as she opened her ice cream sandwich.

Chris reluctantly offered details about Trey's proposal. "I told him yes, if that's what you're wanting to know."

"Hell, I can't tell that you did. You've been on another planet since you got back to my place. Wait a minute. Are you having second thoughts?"

Chris watched the tourists file in and out of the Panda House. There must have been a few thousand people in the zoo that day, and every last one of them must have been standing in line to see those bears that couldn't have cared less about all of the attention.

"To tell you the truth, I don't know what I'm thinking. Personally, I thought I'd be ecstatic and would have at least five bridal magazines inside Chelsea's diaper bag to look at."

"Well, since you don't, I do!" Darcy pulled out two bridal magazines and a wedding planner. "Have you thought about a date yet?"

"Nope."

"Colors?"

"Nope."

"Chris!"

"I'm sorry, but I just don't know what's wrong with me."

Darcy watched Chris' facial expression that had been consistent since she started her interrogation. "If this is the way you're gonna be, then why did you tell him yes?"

Picking up Chelsea from her nap, Chris replied, "I don't know, Darcy. I really don't know." Then she got up and walked toward the Panda House to get in line.

▲

For outsiders, the engagement was moving along quite nicely but, for those on the inside, the entire thing had become quite peculiar. That August, Trey went to see Chris and Chelsea. It hadn't quite been six weeks since they'd last seen each other, and things seemed tense. So Chris tried to spur things along by setting up job interviews for Trey, hoping to facilitate a more expeditious move to Memphis for him. He had a phone interview with the library and was immediately offered a job in its radio production department. Certain that she wouldn't have to deal with Mrs. Withers' nonchalant attitude, Chris was making strides toward her picture-perfect family.

A month later Chris realized Trey was procrastinating about moving to Memphis and had been telling everyone except Chris, his fiancée, that he didn't want to go. Feeling the hesitance and reluctance in Trey's actions, Chris knew there was only one person who would tell her the truth. Darcy.

"Wassuppppp!!!!!!!!!!!!!" Chris screamed into the phone.

"Hey, Lil' Mama!! Where's my godchild? Can she say Darcy yet?"

"Uh, excuse me. I'm fine."

"Don't nobody care about you. Where's that baby?" Darcy insisted.

"In there with Momma. Girl, this is Granny's quality time. Jeopardy doesn't even keep her from the baby. Look, I need to talk to you about something. You have a minute?"

Darcy paused for a few seconds, as she had been anticipating this call. "Sure, what's up?"

"All bullshit aside, does Trey want to come here?"

"Nope." It didn't warrant hesitation.

Disappointed but not surprised, Chris responded, "I figured that."

"Hell, couldn't you tell? He should've been there weeks ago. He told me that he didn't want to move to Memphis because it was too slow. He wanted to stay here. I told him that he needed to tell you as soon as possible, before you made any more arrangements."

"Well, it's too late for that. We got the apartment yesterday, and the phone should've been turned on this afternoon."

"Damn, Boo. What are you going to do?"

"I'll probably go ahead and take the apartment. It's time for me and Pooh to move on."

"Awww, my lil' godbaby. So, how has it been? Are you nuts yet?" Darcy could tell that there was something wrong with Chris.

"It's been cool, I guess. Momma helps out a lot."

ou're okay? You don't sound like yourself. I know that

m too sure about the whole marriage thing when you

here, and you still haven't mentioned anything about it."

"Don't you see why? I've always felt that he was going to bail out on me."

"Don't let that niggah bother you. He's the one that's missing out. Just make sure the judge gets his ass. You know how they get."

"Girl, Trey isn't like that. He'll take care of her." Chris hesitated. "I have something else I need to talk to you about, though."

"What is it?"

"I'm not ready to get into it yet."

"What the hell did you bring it up for then? I hate it when you do that."

"I'll tell you later. I promise. I need to get the baby to bed, so I can call this fucka."

"Please don't clown, Chris. That's part of the problem." Darcy had fucked up. It had slipped.

"Excuse me?" Chris asked with much attitude.

"Look, if you're going to call him, just be kind of cool. Aiight? You two have a child now. He gets so aggravated with your attitude."

"Whatever. I'll call you back in about an hour."

By now, Chris' business with Trey was no longer an issue, and calling him would have to wait until she had gotten her news off her chest. It had been become utterly important to tell some-body—anybody—about what was going on.

6

"Twenty-three-year-old SBF in search of same seeks friendship and possible relationship. Well-educated, attractive, and loves to travel. Must understand that there are two sides to every story."

This ad ran in the Memphis Flyer for almost a month. The first meeting was with a forty-three-year-old white woman who had a son Chris' age and who had awkwardly responded to a seemingly harmless ad for female companionship. The sexual attraction was immediate. It was the first time that she had ever had pussy at her disposal. The woman, not accustomed to pretty, young thangs, began to adore Chris and gave her the love that she had grown to miss ever since she had been away from Trey. But later in the three-month relationship, the woman admitted that she had responded to Chris' ad simply for a quick fuck and was not intending to fall in love with anyone because she already had a lover—a prominent Black doctor who had been too busy to cater to her needs. Thus, she had started searching and had found Chris, a beautiful woman twenty years her junior. Carol, a cross between a hag and poor, white trash, loved Black women. She had once asked Chris if she'd ever watched a Black woman eat a piece of chicken. Baffled but trying not to be offended, Chris told her "no" and that she had never paid any attention to such detail.

a grin on her face, responded, "That's the way they
hat's the way I want them to eat mine."

t comment, but she assumed that she had fit the mold
ьecause their intense physical involvement lasted for three months.

Even though they'd been talking by phone for a couple of days,
Chris met Gayle face-to-face the day after she'd met Carol. By this
time Chris looked forward to responding to the suitors from the
newspaper, and Gayle was the first Black woman to call. They had
spoken on the phone a couple of times before they'd actually met.
Still carrying quite a bit of weight from her pregnancy, Chris was
the prettiest woman that Gayle had lain eyes on in a long time, but
she instantly knew that Chris was out of her league, for Chris lived
on the nicer side of town and had a college degree. Still, Gayle
pursued her anyway. Chris, lonely but flattered by all of the attention, basked in the newness of the gay lifestyle and couldn't wait to
finally be a part of "the life." She had become so smitten with her new
life that Trey's absence and his silence had just passed right on by.

The evening that Gayle first dropped by, Chris didn't bother
about getting dressed or anything. She kept on her nightshirt and
put on a pair of shorts. Chris heard Gayle's car pull up in front of
the house and peeped through the blinds to make sure that it was
her much-anticipated guest. Although she could only see Gayle's
silhouette, Chris had a strange feeling about her new suitor. What am
I doing? "C'mon in," she said, pushing open the wrought-iron door.

"Girl, you sure live a long way out. Hell, I shoulda packed a lunch!"

Finally, Chris could see the face that belonged to the voice that
had been putting her to sleep for the last couple of nights. Gayle
had the most beautiful eyes, passionate and sultry. She had a big,
ghetto booty and, when she passed by, the air smelled absolutely
incredible. Chris peeped out the door and saw that there were
other people in the car.

"I could've met you somewhere," Chris offered. "I know that it is
quite a ways out. Do your friends want to come in?"

"No, I just came by to say hello. I need to get going." Gayle had found some new pussy to conquer. Some fresh pussy. Some smart pussy. "It was nice meeting you," she said, and she was out the door.

"Nice meeting you, too!" Chris yelled down the driveway. Damn, she has a big booty, Chris thought. She was even kind of cute.

The following day Gayle called Chris on every coffee break she had. The chase was on. By the sixth call, Chris was a little annoyed but was enjoying the attention.

"You wanna go out tonight?" Gayle finally asked.

Chris was reluctant to accept because she was waiting to hear from Carol. The previous night, which was the first night they'd ever seen each other, she and Chris got down to their panties, and then Chris told Carol that she was on her period—even though the blood was hardly even there.

"What!" Carol exclaimed. "Why are you just now saying something?"

Blushing, Chris said, "I didn't think I was going to like it."

Anticipating Mother Nature's departure, they'd made a date for the next night, but somehow it had all become contingent upon Carol's plans for the evening.

It was late, and Chris still hadn't heard from Carol. Going into game mode, Chris knew she had nothing to lose by going out with Gayle. So she finally made time for Gayle and tried to mentally prepare herself for whatever came next. As she sat silently on the phone waiting for Gayle to stop bragging about her solos in the choir and the many women that called her house every night, Chris conceded, interjecting, "Sure, I can go. Where are you going to take me?"

"I thought maybe out to dinner and who knows what else."

Gayle only wanted some pussy, and because she was well-seasoned and accustomed to first-timers, she knew that Chris wasn't giving up the goodies.

"What do you mean, who knows what else? You're asking me for a date and don't even know where you're taking me?"

"Well, hell, you wanna go to a hotel afterwards?"

Chris was wishing for that. She didn't know how to suggest something so forward and, at this point in her new life, she wasn't going to either. "I guess we can go. I'll be ready about eight."

"I'll see you then."

Five minutes after that, the phone rang, and it was Carol. "Hey, gal, you ready?" Carol had a tasteless habit of calling women, especially Black women, "gal."

Despite what was definitely socially uncouth, Chris was grinning so damn hard her face was about to break. "Yeah, I'll be over there in a minute." And she was out the door, leaving specific instructions with her mother not to tell Gayle where she was.

Once she'd arrived at Carol's house, Chris was given nothing but the runaround. Carol was supposedly waiting on her son to show up because he and his girlfriend were having some relationship issues. Chris was slouched on the couch with a beer in one hand and the remote in the other when Carol appeared in the doorway completely nude. Walking over to the sliding patio doors to pull the blinds shut, Carol had no shame in showing her sagging physique to a complete stranger. Chris, full of three Coronas by then, had no problem with looking at it.

There's enough time for a quickie, Carol thought as she kissed Chris from the waist up. Her hand was so far into Chris' pants that it felt like Chris was sitting on Carol's arm. Then the phone rang.

"That's probably my son calling to tell me that he's on his way. I'm gonna get it in the back. This'll only take a minute."

Chris sat there and waited for Carol, but she didn't come right back. Enough time passed for Chris to sober up a little and for the fire burning between her legs, and in the fireplace, to slowly turn into a flicker. When Carol returned to the room, she was fully dressed and, without any explanation, she told Chris to leave. "I'll call you tomorrow."

No good-bye kiss or anything. Three months later, Chris found out that Carol had been in the back room all that time talking to her lover and was desperately trying to keep her from coming over. Rejected but still in need of some company, she'd stopped at a pay phone and called Gayle.

"Hello," a groggy voice answered.

"Uh, you mad at me?" There was no response. "Hello, Gayle? You up?"

"Yeah, I'm awake. What the hell happened to you?"

Thinking fast, Chris answered, "I was at my daddy's helping him move into his new house. We're just now finishing up."

"Chris, it's after midnight! You could've called."

"You are mad at me."

"Just a little. I had to cancel out on a friend who had bent over backwards to get us a room at his hotel. That was close to impossible with the Classic going on this weekend."

"I'm sorry." Yes, it was late, but Chris was not ready to go home. She still had some energy and felt like hangin' out awhile. "Well, is it too late to still go out?"

"Hell, yes," Gayle snapped. "But we can, if you want to."

"Cool. Meet me at my mother's house in half an hour."

That night they hung out and went to a fuck-by-the-hour motel. There was a cluster of them off Summer Avenue. It was so damn nasty that the beds were still warm from the couple before them and, in the dark corners where the sidewalks met, the maids stood smoking cigarettes while armed with cans of Lysol and fresh sheets, waiting for the next room to be vacated.

"I'm sorry about this, but all I have on me is a twenty. We've got an hour." Gayle was lying through her teeth. She had just gotten paid but, to pay Chris back for lying, this was the best that she was going to get. Gayle drove around the lot to #12 and stopped the car. The time was 1:05 a.m.

An hour? Chris nervously thought. She didn't even want to spend a second there, but it beat having to go home. When she walked in, she could still smell the sex from the last guests. Swiftly, she ran past the bed and went straight to the bathroom. *What am I doing?* she thought as she squatted over the toilet. She knew nothing about this kind of thing. But the room was paid for, and she had convinced Gayle to get out of bed.

"We don't have but an hour!" Gayle yelled. She wondered what tasting fresh, new pussy was going to be like. Every woman she had been with over the last few months had been ugly, and had slept with more than their share of women. Gayle, like Carol, was only out for a fuck. You find fucks in the newspaper's personal ads. Nothing else.

Chris came out of the bathroom. "I'm sorry. I had to make sure that my period was gone."

"Is it?"

"Yeah."

Gayle walked over to the television to try to get the radio to work. "Damn, can we get some music here? WDIA usually plays some good stuff this time of night. Turn off the light."

The light went off, and Chris spread herself across the bed. Gayle climbed on top of her, and they began kissing. Gayle's kisses were powerful. Not subtle like Carol's. She was on a mission to conquer new pussy. Little did she know, Chris was thinking about Carol the entire time. Gayle's lack of compassion completely turned Chris off, and the end could not come quick enough. With the thrust of Gayle's hips and the pounding of her groin, Chris could not help but have an orgasm. But she never made a sound. Gayle pulled off Chris' shorts and began to lick around the lips of her pussy. Chris wasn't ready for that.

"Wait a minute. What are you doing?"

Gayle looked up and asked, "What?"

"I just got off my period. Isn't that kind of nasty right now?"

"Nope. It'll be all right."

Chris was uncomfortable. Her hips quivered from the touch of Gayle's tongue. "I don't want you to do that. Wait until next time."

"C'mon, I don't mind."

"Well, I do. Please, let's wait."

Gayle was puzzled but respected Chris' wishes. She climbed back on top of Chris and while bumping and grinding against Chris' groin, Gayle, with beads of sweat rolling from her forehead, spontaneously sighed. "I'm too old for this shit." It was exactly two in the morning.

They had five minutes to get their clothes on because a waiting list had formed, and the motel manager was sitting on cloud nine. Every hourly patron had to haul ass out of there at the end of their hour. Chris didn't have time to think about the fact she'd just left a motel with another woman at 2 a.m. She didn't even care about being seen when they got in the car. As they pulled away, she heard the clanking of the wheels on the supply carts as the maids meandered toward #12.

For three months, Gayle and Chris played games while Chris was still in and out of Carol's bed. Phone calls between Gayle and her new "piece" lasted through all hours of the night, but yet, they didn't get along.

Whenever one of them started revealing more than what she wanted the other to know, most of the calls ended in rude, abrupt hang-ups. Days and even weeks would pass without them talking. No love was ever lost, though. Playing the conniving seductress, Chris took sadistic pleasure in inviting Gayle over just so she could watch her dress for a date with another woman. She was also taking advantage of the fact that it sexually aroused Gayle to watch a woman get dressed. The precision in lining the lips and eyes, coupled with Chris' matching bra, panties, thigh-highs and garter belt, moistened Gayle as she throbbed between her legs. Chris had no shame in her full-figured garb, strutting from one side of the room to the other while reminding Gayle that "the real show" was really for Carol. Chris used Gayle as a filler when Carol wasn't around. If Carol happened to surface while Chris was entertaining Gayle, the date was instantly over—no matter where they were. Her mind—caught up in endless games—might have belonged to Gayle, but Chris' body had Carol's name written all over it.

▲

Christmas soon came and was anything but joyous and festive for Chris. Instead of helping Chelsea enjoy her first Christmas, Chris was planning a romantic time with Carol, and despite the fact that they'd spent the whole week before December 25th together, Chris ended up involved in more drama than she'd ever seen in any soap opera.

In the prior months Carol had wined and dined Chris, bought her a whole new wardrobe and introduced her to the white lesbian club scene in Memphis by taking her to WKRB in Midtown. Carol wouldn't be caught dead in a Black club with Chris on her arm and, to her amazement, Chris had actually enjoyed herself. Sheryl Crow's first big hit "All I Wanna Do" blasted from the speakers at least twice that night and, as it was truly her coming out, Chris had adopted it as her anthem.

Amidst that, there were other problems brewing. Carol always made sure that Chris was drunk before they fucked so the encounter might be mutually pleasurable for both of them. She may have fed her and clothed her but, outside of that, Carol knew they had nothing in common. Chris, aware that there were lots of secrets, dared not pry into the private life that Carol closely guarded. Carol would disappear for days without calling Chris and would never have an explanation for it. The only words that always saved her were "I love you, Chris," for Chris often needed reassurance that at least one somebody gave a damn about her. Carol had said those words so many times, however, that she had started believing it herself. A seasoned lesbian, this woman walked all over Chris and was allowed to do it.

One morning Chris, on a whim, drove by Carol's house and found her car still in the driveway. This was after she had told Chris that she was going out of town. Afraid of stopping by unannounced, Chris dashed to a pay phone to call her and blasted Carol for the obvious lie. Carol could never get the entire lie straight, and Chris ended up saying that she was tired of being used just for sex. But wouldn't you know it? On this particular day, Carol had a house guest who had picked up the other extension and heard everything. The shit hit the fan. That explained why the car was in the driveway. The unsuspecting doctor, fearful of someone associating her with a white lesbian, parked her car in the garage whenever she visited Carol. Chris heard the echo in the phone line and surmised that someone was on the other end, but she didn't say a word about it. Within seconds, Carol was engaged in a heated argument with her secret lover.

"Chris, you've made me hurt the woman I love!" she yelled, and then she smashed the receiver in its cradle.

To be vindictive, Carol subsequently told Chris' mother all about her daughter's new ventures, including how they had met and how many times they had bumped pussies. Imagine this. Your mother finding out that you're gay from a white redneck woman that you've seen naked on what now seemed to be too many occasions.

The only comment that Mrs. Desmereaux made to Carol was, "I know that my daughter has better taste than this in women. At least she got that much from her daddy."

Paranoid about who knew what and how they knew it, Chris had never talked with anyone about what she'd been doing. She'd never thought about how anyone would take it. The only person who was open-minded enough to hear it, digest it, and analyze it was Darcy. Chris recognized, though, that she was due a good cussing out because she'd never called Darcy back from the last time they'd spoken.

"You know what? Caller ID is something else. I've been dodging folks right and left, and then I look down at the box and see that it's yo' ass finally callin' me back after, what is it now? Almost four months?"

Chris was ready. "Go on, let me have it. I know I'm wrong."

"Damn right! And then you've had me waitin' in suspense at that! What the hell is up?"

"I've been seeing this woman." Before she knew it, she'd said it.

"Well, sometimes counseling is good. You need a neutral party." Darcy, a psychology major, wasn't listening to Chris. "What kind of therapist is she?"

A lump had formed in Chris' throat, but swallowing had become cumbersome. This was the first person she'd ever shared her secret with and, although Darcy was very open-minded, Chris didn't know what to expect. "No, sweetie. You're missing me. I'm seeing a woman."

"Aw, shit, Chris." Darcy's mouth was wide open. "How, I mean. What? Well, why? Have you done it with her?"

"I guess so."

"What the hell do you mean, you guess so? Either you slept with her, or you didn't!"

"Yes, I did. Now I think I'm into something that I don't want to get out of."

"Is this a passing thing? I mean, you've always been an exploratory bitch. Is this just 'something to do' as you always say?"

"I don't think so. It feels different. My heart feels different, and so does my mind. I think I finally understand why I haven't had much to say about my engagement."

Darcy was stumped. So many questions raced through her mind. What about the times Chris and Trey had fucked in her basement? Or the times when they had fucked in the empty bedrooms? Or the times when they had gone out to some deserted field and had fucked in the car? What about the numerous times they had fucked in the basement of the Methodist house where Chris used to live? What about all the guys in the dormitory? But the only question that could roll off her tongue, though, was, "So what's she like?"

"She's forty-three."

"Aiight. You've always liked 'em older."

"Um, she has a son my age."

"Okay. What else?"

"That's about it. Of course, I'm not her first."

"I would hope not. Does she know about Trey?"

"Yeah. She keeps insisting that I don't know what I want just yet, that I'm too new at the whole thing."

"I can see some validity in that. Can I ask you something?"

A question crossed her mind that could affect everything that would be said from that moment on.

"What?"

"You realize that you have basically told me that you cheated on Trey, don't you? This shit has got to be heavy, if you did that."

"Well, you know, Darcy. I think that he has made his position on us very clear. Don't you think? A real man would have called me himself and told me what you did. Besides, I still haven't talked to him."

"You didn't call him either?"

"No. Have you talked with him anymore?"

"Actually, I have. He was over here the other night. Surprisingly, he didn't say anything to me about you or the baby. I almost think that he was afraid to."

"What?" Chris was astonished. "What do you mean, he was afraid?"

"Girl, you know how you get. You would've been on the first thing smoking, trying to kick his ass, and you know this. He's probably going through his own thing, just like you're going through yours. I'd let him be for the moment because you've got some pretty big shit to deal with."

Chris thought hard about what she had just been told. Trey was afraid of her, afraid of commitment, afraid of everything, and when she needed him most, he was beginning to walk away. Now there seemed to be no hope of having a perfect family for Chelsea. Quickly, she realized that maybe this was a blessing in disguise. The longer he stayed away, the more time she would have to "express herself" and find out more about the new lifestyle she'd been experimenting with. Chris' mood changed, and she remembered that there was something she'd forgotten to tell Darcy, and it wasn't that there was more than one woman involved. "Not to change the subject, but there is something I forgot to tell you about Carol."

"What? She's rich."

"No, she's white."

"WHAT! Now, Chris…"

Chris was expecting that because Darcy hated interracial relationships. Managing to cut Darcy off before she had time to get worked up, Chris interjected, "I have to go. Your godchild is crying!" And she slammed the phone down.

"Damn, Chris, the least you could do, since you're fucking a woman, is fuck somebody Black. Damn you…"

Realizing that Chris had hung up, Darcy looked to the ceiling and said, "Damn, Chris. Damn."

7

Waiting for Trey to get his act together, Chris kept her new lifestyle a secret from almost everyone in her family—except for her sister who had already investigated Chris' suspicious behavior months before and concluded that Chris was indeed "dyking." Iysha even tried to talk with Trey to see where his head was, but it was to no avail. He simply had nothing to say and still didn't ask about Chelsea. To the family's dismay, Trey never got his shit together, and Chris was left with the memories of what it was like living without a dad at home. She'd never wanted that for Chelsea, but those were the cards that Chris was being dealt. Together, her parents had made many mistakes in their upbringing, and Chris often wondered which of those same mistakes she'd make alone.

The first time that Chris brought home a B on her report card, her mother's reply was, "Thank God. At least you're not perfect!" There was really no way to respond to that comment because she had brought home straight As every marking period since she was in the first grade. To keep her mother happy, not only did Chris keep making the Bs, but she also sprinkled in a few Cs and Ds to go along with them.

Mr. Desmereaux then commented, "See what you did! This girl ain't gonna be fit for shit! Her grades are all fucked up, and now we gotta pay for her to go to school!"

Chris never got to go to any of the after-school functions that semester because she stayed on punishment so much for her grades.

One afternoon while Chris was reading a simple juvenile fiction book from the high school library, her grandmother yelled at her for reading too much. "Every time I see ya, ya gotta damn book in ya hand! Put that book down!" From that point on, Chris never opened another book in her grandmother's house.

Chris did the honor society thing and got more respect than any other student. Her teachers adored her for her determination and quiet, competitive spirit. They gave her books to read and famous quotes to remember and, whenever there was a special event coming up, she was the first that was invited to attend. Still, despite the lack of encouragement from her family, Chris graduated from high school with honors and was offered full scholarships from both Princeton University and Howard University. Having gone to a predominantly white high school, Chris felt deprived of her culture and her ancestors. Although Princeton was an Ivy League school and carried one of the best academic reputations in the world, Chris chose to attend Howard because it would ultimately define who she wanted to become.

A first-generation college student, Chris tried desperately to win the affection and attention of her mother and father. There were never any hugs, never any kisses. Whenever Chris did excel in her studies while in primary school, it was her teachers who praised her and commended her on her performance. Those hugs from her teachers were better than life itself. She looked forward to seeing them every morning and occasionally greeted them with little thoughts of kindness. Chris never realized the attraction to women that she had developed. She only knew that the smell of their perfumes and the gentleness in their strides caused her to perform exceedingly well in their presence, and to her, that was normal.

Carlos and Ora Desmereaux got married when they were still in high school. Ora was an honor student but was asked to leave when it was revealed that she was pregnant. In those days, it was a disgrace for a girl to walk the halls with a bloated belly and no husband. As the principal rudely put it, "It compromised the integrity of the senior class." Pressure from both sides of the family came almost instantly. They had to get married, despite Carlos' reputation as a "ho." Even on his wedding night, he had slipped out while Ora slept. He hooked up with an old girlfriend for about an hour and managed to creep back into bed before Ora awakened. Knowing that a wife and a baby would never slow Carlos down, every girl in the neighborhood had a thing for, or had a history with, the handsome drum major. Ora Desmereaux graduated from night school a year later with Chris on her hip and another offspring growing in her womb. She miscarried after the first trimester.

Over the next three years, Carlos Desmereaux maintained his reputation as a "ho" and managed to keep Ora pregnant. Of the following two pregnancies, only one survived—a girl named Iysha Michelle. A proud father in the beginning, the girls accompanied Carlos to his female friends' homes. That is, until they learned to talk and communicated to Ora about their daily outings. Carlos was lowdown and complacent, too. He wouldn't even change Iysha's diapers, letting her sit in shit until his wife got home. They did the food stamp thing for a while, but they still had to take in some extras from family and friends. It was hard, but they managed to stay afloat. Carlos made half-ass attempts at trying to be a father but always fell short when it came down to the nitty-gritty.

One afternoon Chris, when she was four, came in the house crying because a little girl from down the street kept hitting her and taking her toys. Every time Chris came back in the house her father sent her right back out the door and told her not to come back until she had all of her toys in her hand. On her way out the door, Chris grabbed a big, red plastic baseball bat that her grandfather had given her, intending to beat the girl's ass and take her toys back. Instead, when Chris got ready to swing, the girl took the bat and beat the shit out of Chris. After all the sobs and bruises, the girl kept the bat and added it to her collection of Chris' toys. Carlos just stood there watching. The next week he moved his family out of the projects.

A playa to the end, Carlos wasn't ashamed when his women called the house, nor was he ashamed to let them drive the car that he and his wife shared. Most of the time he nonchalantly let shit happen without any regard for his family's feelings. After two separations, Ora felt that maybe her life with Carlos was worth another try. He shared an apartment with one of his old high school buddies, and they simply ran a cat house for all their friends. Carlos had reached the point where holidays didn't mean anything to him. He would show up on Christmas Eve at 5:30 p.m. with $50 for his daughters' Christmas gifts. Ora knew that he was making over $30,000 at Coca-Cola, but she never hounded him for child support. She quietly took the money and then reimbursed her mother for the things that she had already paid for. Carlos did that shit at Easter and at the beginning of the school year. It never bothered him that he was so trifling.

Ora visited him one Sunday after church because he, Chris, and Iysha had cooked taco pie for her. It was the children's innocent attempt at helping their parents reconcile. While the girls were finishing up dinner, Ora started rambling through Carlos' things, just as she'd done when they were together. Some loose change, old receipts, and past-due bills were the usual items that she found. But this time she found some other disturbing things—a bill from a pediatrician and an 8x10 portrait of a baby girl. Ora quietly closed the dresser drawer and went into the kitchen where Carlos and their daughters were. She sat down at the space the children had set for her and never made eye contact with Carlos.

Chris asked, "Momma, what's wrong? Why you so quiet?"

Ora smiled and asked for the salad bowl. "Guess what, girls?" Ora chuckled. It was all she could do to keep from bursting into tears. "Y'all got a little sister."

Chris' and Iysha's mouth dropped open. And Carlos? He was choking on a nacho chip.

Gasping for air while reaching for a glass of Kool-Aid, Carlos grunted, "No, you don't! Ya Momma don't know what she talkin' 'bout!" He scowled at Ora, gesturing for her to move to the other room. "You ain't got no other sister," he said calmly.

"Bullshit," Ora uttered. "What the hell you doin' with that doctor's bill then? I know damn well you haven't taken my children to the doctor. Oh, my bad. You took them to the free clinic while you were takin' some other bitch's baby to a real damn doctor."

"Ora, we need to talk, but not in front of them."

"We ain't got shit to talk about." Ora got up from the table and gathered the children's belongings. "Lying ass muthafucka! Ain't never been able to keep ya dick to yourself!"

She hated the fact that her girls had to hear this, but it was finally time for them to know why their daddy was never around. By the time Ora got the bags packed, the girls were already at the door. Chris was devastated, and Iysha knew that she had been bumped as "the baby."

"C'mon, Ora. Don't do this in front of the babies. Please don't!" Carlos whined as he ran behind Ora.

Out of breath and with her eyes full of tears, Ora turned and slapped Carlos with all of her might. "How dare you say that to me after all that you've already done? You don't do shit for them unless somebody makes you, and any man that has to be made to take care of his own flesh and blood—his own children—ain't even a man."

That was the last time that Chris and Iysha ever spent the weekend with their father as adolescents. The following Monday Ora filed for child support and eventually settled for $50 a week for both girls.

Carlos showed up for the important stuff like the honors' programs and the graduations, but he only stayed a hot minute. Immediately after Iysha's graduation, Carlos asked for her diploma so that he could stop paying child support for her. But the judge wasn't having it. New laws required him to keep paying it until Iysha turned twenty-one. Carlos went almost a year without speaking to Ora or his children, blaming the girls for his pitfalls and hang-ups. It didn't stop him from fucking because he had two more babies before Chris graduated from college.

After her relationship with Carlos, Ora decided that she needed to get a grip. She put her daughters first by buying them the best of everything. The three of them spent each weekend in the mall and did everything possible to forget about Carlos. Chris quietly missed her dad but dared to ever say it in front of her mother. She often remembered the empty promises, particularly the one where she had waited for her daddy to come over and teach her how to ride her first ten-speed bike. She had waited so long that by sunset she had taught herself how to ride it and, despite the bruises and scrapes on her knees, he had never apologized for not showing up.

▲

Southland Greyhound Park was the hottest place in town for fun. The atmosphere, divided into three sections—the Clubhouse, the Paddock Club, and the Kennel Club—embraced every social class. The Clubhouse was air-conditioned but only in sections. Everybody was welcomed there. Behind it was the Paddock Club. It wasn't as crowded as the Clubhouse, and there was a bar and some monitors to view the races. Then there was the socially elite spot, the Kennel Club. Dinner jackets and ties were mandatory, and every table was covered with the finest linen. Waiters in bow ties and cummerbunds provided first-class service in the members-only establishment, and guests had the best seats in the house. A woman was sure to find an available bachelor with some loot in there. But with all the class and personality Ora possessed, she ended up meeting a bum from The Clubhouse.

Pete Caldwell lived in his car—a car that he built. His family was from Sugar Ditch, Tunica County, Mississippi—the poorest county in the country. He never bathed nor did he ever brush his teeth. There was no culture, no luster, nothing. But Ora Desmereaux fell in love with him. She cooked him those big brontosaurus burgers and those ghetto salmon croquettes with onions and green peppers hanging out of them. Whenever there was a tray of six chicken breasts, Pete automatically got three.

Ora purchased her first home for her and her daughters. They sacrificed a big Christmas so that she could save up some money. After years of sharing a room, Iysha and Chris finally had their own bedrooms. And for the first time in their lives, the two girls were allowed to go to school with the kids from the neighborhood so that they'd be with relatives after school. They had spent previous years attending schools that were across town from where they lived. The three women finally had a place of their own—no left-up toilet seats, no need to cover up, and a sense of love and affection that had much to be desired.

Chris was notorious for walking around partially nude, and Iysha followed in her big sister's footsteps. One morning, after Ora had come in from the dog track, Iysha got up to go to the bathroom. She heard voices in the front room, but she didn't see anyone in the dark. Figuring that it was Pete and her mother, Iysha went on to bed. The next afternoon Chris asked Iysha if she had been hearing noises over in the night, and Iysha explained that Pete and Ora had been sitting up all night giggling like two schoolkids. Soon after, the girls realized that Pete was leaving the house just before dawn, or basically just before their alarm clocks went off.

"Y'all need to be better about cleanin' this house," Ora scolded. "I want this house spotless by the time I get home."

Chris and Iysha had been waiting until 4:25 to clean up knowing their mother got off work at 4:30. Ora usually got home about 4:45, and the chores were never finished. After their mother's harsh words, the girls started cleaning up at 4:15 instead. One afternoon Chris decided to start with her mother's bathroom but was not prepared for what she found. Underneath the cabinet, carefully hidden in the back corner, were a man's razor and some clean underwear. There was a pick for that big ass Jheri-curl Pete had and a couple of pairs of socks. Ora had moved his shit in and had been letting him spend most of the night in bed with her. Within a month's time, Pete became a permanent fixture.

Chris agonized over this stranger that had moved into her home. Hell, had she known that they were running a homeless shelter, she could have invited a number of her classmates to live with her. Ora gradually started spending less time at home and more time at work or either at the dog track. Relatives began to realize that Pete was unemployed and never intended to get a job. Chris and Iysha were pissed because if they didn't have jobs, they didn't get to eat.

During her senior year in high school, Chris got to a point where she couldn't take anymore. Pete's tired ass was at home all day while her mother slaved at work. Then when she got home, he expected her to cook while he hung out at the pool hall. And the icing on the cake were the noises he made when he and Ora had sex. He sounded like a damn bear, acting as if he were out in the wilderness and was mating for the first time. Ora knew her children heard them because, whenever she emerged from her bedroom, she could never look at them in the face.

Remaining focused on getting into a good school, Chris did

nothing but concentrate on her grades. This was her final chance to get her act together and break free from a city that she'd come to hate. She didn't allow anything to bother her. Anything she was asked to do, she quickly did. Her position as editor of the yearbook kept her busy, so she didn't spend much time at home. Then one evening when she came home late, all the shit started.

"I thought I told you to do the laundry and the dishes before you went to bed last night?" Ora snapped.

"What?" Chris replied unknowingly. It was almost nine o'clock, and the only thing that had been on her mind for the past fourteen hours was getting those last pages of the yearbook off to the printer. She had missed all of her classes that day but had promised her teachers that she would be on task the following day. Dragging her weary body to the bedroom to place down her books, Chris passed right by her mother.

"Excuse me?" Ora said sarcastically. "What do you mean, what? Don't forget who you talkin' to, young lady! Been runnin' 'round with those white kids all day and then you get here and forget your place!"

Chris was so tired that her eyes were almost blood red. Pete was in the bedroom where he usually was, and he hadn't done a damn thing all day. Dishes were stacked in the sink, and dirty laundry was still laying on the kitchen floor. Iysha was out of town with the Biology club. The students were taking their annual trip to the Huntsville Space Center, and they weren't due back until after midnight.

"Did you hear what I said, Chris?"

"Yes, ma'am, I heard you. Momma. I told you last night that I had a busy day today and that I wouldn't be home until late tonight. I was up all last night working on my term paper."

"I don't care what you had to do. Your responsibilities to this house come first. You're grounded until whenever. No parties, no dances, no afterschool stuff, nothing. And you better not call your daddy and call yourself telling on me because not only will I beat your ass about it, but I will also add another month to your punishment! Do you understand?"

Chris clicked. "What do you mean? Momma, you know I have to be at those functions. I'm one of the officers."

"So."

"So? That's all you can say to me is so? That trifling ass bastard has been here all day long, and you jump on my case about doing some housework? You work Iysha and me like mules, and he gets to lie on his ass all day? Do you actually think that's fair? Hell, he won't even take out the garbage! He doesn't do shit for you, Momma. You're even too embarrassed to take him out to dinner because he eats like a damn pack of wild dogs. And where are your friends, Momma? They're sitting back shaking their heads at you and wondering why you're settling for that sack of shit!"

Ora swarmed on Chris like flies to shit and started pounding her fists into her firstborn's face. Chris didn't have much energy left to fight back. Remembering to never strike her mother, Chris managed to push her mother back into a corner and scrambled to the front door.

"If you leave, you better take yo' shit with you!"

Chris gained some composure. "Momma, I thought this was our house. I thought this was something just for us. You moved him in here and..."

"And what?" Ora sobbed. Something more was going on, and Ora knew that she was wrong for what she had done. But she never had any intention of apologizing for it. "Go on and say what you have to say."

Wiping the water from her eyes and nose, Chris whimpered, "You just moved him in here. You never bothered to ask us if it was okay."

"Since when do I have to ask your permission?"

"It's not about permission. It's about the fact that you moved a complete stranger in with us. You had no regard for our feelings about that. How do you honestly expect for Iysha or me to be loving to anybody if we have to deal with two parents who care more about the person they're sleeping with than they do their own kids?"

"Girl, don't you know that I do all I can for you and your sister? I buy you nice things and take you places…"

"Momma, it's not about the material things all the time. How many times have you asked me how my day was? Or did I enjoy school? You never ask me anything like that. All I want from you is your love and not your presents or money." Chris started sobbing uncontrollably. "I just want you to love me like you love that man back there. I know you hug him, and I've even heard you ask him how his useless day was."

Ora never commented. She simply went to her room and closed her door. Chris left the house that night and went to live with Carlos for a couple of weeks. He was responsible for getting Ora to take Chris back in because he was too damn lazy to take her back and forth to school every day. Once back at home, the routine was still the same, and Pete still didn't have a job.

Chris wholeheartedly believed that she didn't need anyone—even though she was going through something that had begun while she was with those relatives on the other side of town. In the beginning, the matter required an adult's immediate attention, but Chris knew that she wasn't particularly ready for the potential fallout from it. Child molestation wasn't that big of a deal back then, so she just let it go. When she and Iysha changed schools, the problem was temporarily nipped in the bud.

Iysha and Chris clashed because Iysha was more of a street person than Chris. On the other hand, Chris was a bookworm and brilliant. Iysha stayed with her mother long enough after high school to make some money and eventually convinced Carlos to let her live with him since he was always laid up over some woman's house.

The money got to be so good that she decided not to go to college. Chris, however, opted to leave the city of Memphis in search of a better life.

Carlos took the revelation about his daughter being gay the hardest. One evening when he had stopped by, Chris was on the phone arguing with Carol. After she'd slammed down the phone, Carlos and Chris sat in his car and he asked her why she was doing what she was doing with women. "Why not?" she responded. He, of all people, started preaching to her about what was right and what was wrong. Chris knew that his ego was crushed. But so what? Her father was the epitome of a dog and, when surrounded by other dogs of the same kennel, he bragged about his sexual prowess and didn't care who heard him. "Chris, you ain't no bad-lookin' woman! Why you gotta do this?"

"You want to know why I do this?"

"Baby, I ain't tryin' to get in yo' business, but this just ain't right. These kind of relationships are the most vicious around."

Chris glared out the window of her father's sports car. Thoughts of her father's women from her childhood ran through her memory. The phone calls, the love letters. All of those things Chris knew about. "Daddy, did you ever care that I saw you with any of those other women?"

"What women?"

This is sad, Chris thought. *He doesn't even remember any of them.* "The ones that you flaunted in front of me and my sister. The ones that called our house and taunted Momma about you being their man. The ones that you said were coworkers. The ones that you said were just friends. Should I go on?" she screamed. "I can, you know!"

Scratching his head, Mr. Desmereaux took a deep breath. He never knew that he was being watched so closely. "Chris, those women didn't mean anything to me. Sometimes men and women…"

"Look, don't kick that shit to me. I'm grown, now, and I know. Okay? I know! For God's sake, Daddy, you've got a baby by a woman that is only four years older than me!"

"What do you want me to say, Chris? You want me to say I'm sorry?"

"No, because you don't mean it."

"Is there anything I can say to make you understand? I mean, why don't you just find you a good, young man or something?"

"They don't exist anymore. The mold was broken the day before you were born."

Chris' daddy laughed. "I knew that something was wrong with your ass when…Never mind," he snapped.

Chris then laughed to herself. She never thought that she would be having this discussion with her father. "Daddy, the only thing you need to know is that for as long as I can remember, I only wanted to be just like you. I can remember when I was little, I used to stand in front of the toilet and try to pee like you. When you were at work, I used to put on your shoes and walk around the house in them until you got home. The first time I kissed a boy, I hoped that he'd smell as you did before you went off to work. Like fresh toothpaste and Old English." Chris started crying and refused to look in her father's direction. "I loved Trey because he was everything that you weren't. I tried to mold him by buying nice clothes and cologne for him. Unlike you, he respected my dreams and me. He listened when I needed an ear. He hugged me—even when I didn't want a hug. You never did that. True, he's naive, but he was there. You weren't. He wasn't like the man I discovered you really were. But like you and Momma, he walked out on a relationship without trying to fix it and without any regard for his child. I like the touch of a woman, her fragrance, her body, and what frightens me is that I felt like this even when I was with Trey. I don't yet know why I felt like this, but it's a feeling that I've come to enjoy. I've got my own problems understanding why I'm going through this, but that's for me to do. Not you, and not Momma. Maybe it's a passing phase. All I know is that I've been battling this for a long time, and now I want to find out if there's some happiness in it. It's hard enough for me to deal with this, so I just ask that you let me do so without having to deal with you and your hang-ups about it. I don't know what or who I'm looking for, but if I want to get some peace, I have to find out. I'm not into the having-more-than-one-woman thing because that reminds me so much of you, and that really hurts. I don't blame you for me feeling this way, but you've got your share in it."

"You know, Chris, some things aren't worth trying to save. That's what happened with Ora and me. Live a little longer, and you'll see what I mean. I didn't know that you felt this way."

"You've never asked. You know something else?"

"What's that?"

"I'll acknowledge you. I'll even grieve for you when you die. But never expect me to respect you. That's something you haven't earned from me." Having said that, she got out of the car, and months passed before she spoke to him again.

With a soul thirsty for compassion, Chris turned to Gayle for comfort.

8

Weeks later, Chris was so sick that she couldn't even take care of herself—let alone the baby. Ora came to get Chelsea, giving her daughter some much-needed time to find herself and to think about trying to work things out with Trey. She'd gotten a job substitute teaching and only went to work and came straight home. She had no social life and steered clear of developing one. Even though Gayle would call to check on her and usually offered to come by, Chris didn't want to see her. Finally, after days of sitting inside with the blinds tightly shut, she'd accepted Gayle's offer.

"You been sittin' here in the dark?" Gayle asked as she opened the blinds. "You got it smelling so stuffy in here."

Chris never said a word as she continued resting on a stack of down pillows. The TV was watching her.

"I suppose you gonna just lie there feeling sorry for yourself." Gayle sat down next to her, drinking in her presence. Chris was the most beautiful woman that she had ever seen, and it actually made her feel bad that Chris was so sick. She knew that Chris had some class because her mattresses didn't squeak—the beds of all her other women did. Freshly ironed and crisp, the sheets even looked expensive, and the pillows felt like what royalty might have slept on. Gayle felt that she could love Chris, but Chris would not let her. "Have you eaten anything? If not, I can fix you something."

"No, thank you," Chris whispered. She got up from the bed to go to the bathroom, and Gayle noticed that Chris had dropped a lot of weight.

"Are you sure you're not really sick or something?"

"I'm fine," she mumbled. Chris sat on the toilet and thought. She didn't want anyone around her right now. After days of refusing to see the doctor, Chris had finally made an appointment and had gone earlier in the day. She had the stomach flu, and it was complicated by emotional distress caused by the relationships she'd gotten herself into. Chris was not hurt by Carol's infidelity but instead by the revelation of the lies, and she hated being caught in other people's drama. That was killing her. Chris was trying to love a woman, hoping that she wouldn't lie to her as her father had during her childhood. But Carol did. Chris' father did not love her enough to always tell her the truth and, apparently, Carol didn't either. Daddy always lied to help himself, not realizing the hurt he caused someone else, Chris thought. You just don't hurt the ones you love.

"Gayle, you can go. I'm just going to get back in the bed."

Gayle didn't answer her. Chris heard pots and pans in the kitchen, but was too weak to make it down the hallway. Instead, she got back in bed and resumed watching television.

Within ten minutes, Gayle emerged from the hallway with a bowl of soup and a glass of water. "You really need to eat. Your breath is beginning to stink."

Chris just smiled…for the first time in weeks. She sat up in the bed and instead of handing the bowl to Chris, Gayle began spoon-feeding her. With every motion, Gayle and Chris looked into each other's eyes. Gayle was ready to love her. She was eager to enter into this new world, and she was ready to heal Chris' wounds.

"Do you want me to stay the night with you?" she asked.

"For what?" Chris snapped.

Gayle was caught off guard. She knew Chris needed someone there with her. "To stay here with you…"

"No. If I need a baby-sitter, I'll give you a buzz."

"Are you going to let some bitch, a white one at that, get to you?"

"You don't understand. It doesn't have shit to do with some bitch. You'd never understand, and that's good enough reason for you not to be here. Why even subject yourself to this attitude?" Chris rolled over and covered her face with the blankets. "Lock the door on your way out."

Gayle took the dishes back into the kitchen, washed them, and put them back in their respective places. She let herself out and didn't speak to Chris anymore for almost a month.

That night, when Chris heard her door close, she began crying—sometimes even wailing, wishing that Gayle wouldn't have done as she had asked.

Within four weeks, Chris had lost close to thirty pounds. Her weight loss rejuvenated her spirits, and she was ready to face the world again. But not before making an apology.

"May I speak to Gayle?"

"What do you want?" Gayle snapped.

Chris sucked up her pride. "I'm sorry. I know I was wrong. I just needed to go through that alone. Thank you for being there for me."

Gayle paused. "Did you ever start eating? You were beginning to look anorexic," she joked.

"Gradually. Still not eating as much as I used to. Why don't you come over tonight? We can order pizza or something?"

"I'll think about it. I'm getting ready to go to church right now, though. I really need to be getting off this phone."

"Church on a Thursday night?"

"Yeah, I gotta go." And she hung up.

Chris was so pissed off about Gayle not wanting to see her that she didn't care whether she ever heard from her again. She went ahead and ordered the pizza for Chelsea and her.

About an hour later, Chris heard a faint knock coming from the front room. The closer she got to the hallway she realized that there was someone at her door. It was almost midnight.

"Who is it?"

"Gayle."

She hesitantly opened the door. "Yes, what are you doing here?"

"Uh, you did invite me over for pizza."

"Girl, puh-leeze. That was before you claimed to have to go to church."

"Chris, I have responsibilities to my choir. I..."

"Whatever. C'mon in." Chris led her to the bedroom and pointed to the pizza box. "It's cold."

"I can heat it up, can't I?"

Gayle glanced at Chris' ass. She had dropped weight in all the right places. Gayle couldn't wait.

"That's on you."

Gayle went to the kitchen and warmed her food. When she got back to the bedroom, Chris was back in the bed.

"Don't eat all of it because I need it for my lunch tomorrow."

Chris' bitchiness was creeping up. There were only three slices left.

"I'll give you some lunch money."

"I don't want lunch money from you. Just don't eat all my shit up!"

Gayle lost her appetite and put the pizza down. After a long night at choir rehearsal where attitudes flare and feelings get hurt, she really needed the company that night, but not at this expense. She started taking her shoes off.

"What the fuck are you doing? You ain't staying here tonight."

"Chris, it's late, and I really don't feel like driving home tonight."

"So!"

Gayle was too tired to argue. She got her things and left.

About twenty minutes after Gayle left, the phone rang. It was Darcy.

"Chris?"

"What?"

"You sleep?"

"Nope. What's up? What are you doing up so late?"

"I need to talk to you about Trey."

"Don't you have anything else better to waste your long distance money on?"

"It's important."

"Look, Darcy, I'm not in the mood for this…"

"Just listen, will you please?"

Chris' phone beeped. Who the hell, she thought. "Hold on, Darcy." She pushed the flash button. "Hello."

"Do you expect everyone to kiss your high and mighty ass? I get so tired of you dogging me out—no matter what I try to do for you!"

"Fuck you, Gayle." And she calmly clicked back over. "I'm back, Darcy."

"Chris, Trey is seeing someone else."

Chris paused for a minute. "And?" she said coldly.

"Have you talked to him at all?"

"Nope. And now that you mention it, I really don't want to."

"Well, that's not all."

Chris figured that it couldn't get any worse. "C'mon, Darcy, I'm already in a fucked up mood." The phone beeped again. "Damn! Hold on!" She punched the flash button. "Hello!"

"Chris, please let me come over. I'm tired. I really am."

Gayle got nothing but a dial tone.

"Sorry about that, girl. Now what else has the Almighty Trey done?"

"This girl…She's got a baby."

Chris sunk to the floor. Trey had not called in over four months. He had not sent any money to help out with Chelsea. He had completely cut himself off from Chris and their daughter.

Darcy continued, "He's been picking the baby up and taking her to school and shit. Has he been doing anything for Chelsea?"

"No." There was a knock at the door. "Look, Darcy, someone is at my door."

"At this hour?"

"Yeah, it's probably my neighbor. I'll have to talk to you tomorrow."

"Okay. But Chris, you need to call him." And then in one of those "I told you so" tones, "You should've taken his ass to court!"

"If you've got to make a man take care of his children, then he isn't a man. My daddy's ass has been in and out of court for child support. Need I say more?"

"Girl…"

The knocks were louder and constant, one coming right behind the other. "I have to go." She hung up the phone, knowing who was on the other side. Chris cracked the door.

"I ran out of quarters, and I knew that you wouldn't take a collect call from me."

Chris laughed quietly to herself, unlocked the chain, and let Gayle in. Before Gayle could step foot onto the carpet, Chris grabbed her and kissed her. She hugged Gayle as tightly as she could and, as she wept, her soul crept open.

They never even made it to the bedroom. Gayle dropped to her knees and began circling Chris' waist with urgent, persistent kisses, kisses filled with the hurt and emotional scars they both kept securely tucked away inside. But this time her tattered soul opened as she massaged Chris' every curve. Beneath the floral print of Gayle's knit dress, Chris could feel the rhythmic vibration of her heart racing as her lips, slightly ajar, softly caressed Gayle's smooth ebony skin. Her lungs ballooned, her chest almost exploded with every deep breath as she inhaled the intoxicating scent of Gayle's enticing perfume. Returning a passion fueled by acceptance and unspoken understanding, the two began an intimate, intricate lover's dance that would last until the early morning hours. It was a sensual tango, excreting a symphony of latent emotions that would ultimately define their strange relationship.

After that night Chris realized that she still wasn't emotionally ready for Gayle. But, on the contrary, Gayle was ready to give her heart and soul to Chris. Chris, however, was content with a midnight creep, a little "something to do" every now and then. That meant no commitment and no questions, a perfect arrangement because Gayle had been spending time with someone else anyway when Chris first got sick. Whenever Chris started tripping, Marsha Denton was always a welcomed change for Gayle.

9

lways in need of attention from somebody, Chris still flirted with men. It gave her an assurance that maybe some of them could still be trusted. At the school where she worked, there was a self-proclaimed minister that had befriended her and offered some "spiritual guidance" to assist with her dilemmas. An older man, he had become her only trustworthy male friend, and she thoroughly enjoyed his company. One of his daughters was Chris' age and had recently been crowned Miss Fort Valley State. Her picture was featured in *Ebony* and, at work, all of the teachers boasted and bragged about Mr. Mitchell being such a family man. Letting her guard down, Chris made the mistake of telling him that she was gay. He, as most arrogant men, felt that he could reform her. A respected member of the staff, Mr. Mitchell maintained his professionalism until the day he invited her to his house.

Well, the family man asked Chris for a fuck. She and Gayle hadn't spoken in days, and loneliness had become a constant companion. So there wasn't anything to lose. She didn't think about any consequences. None whatsoever.

Two weeks later, Chris had that feeling again, the same feeling she'd had when she carried that watermelon on her back that August; her saliva had regained that metallic taste almost overnight. Telling Mr. Mitchell—Rev. Mitchell—of her situation, he suddenly lost his religion, screaming, "Pregnant!!! What the hell you mean you're pregnant? Ain't no way you can be pregnant with my baby. I'm sterile…swear to God I'm sterile, Chris! You have got to be out of your fucking mind!" Later, however, this "sterile" man of God decided to give her money for an abortion. "Just in case, you understand, just in case," he mumbled feebly. Her mother and Darcy both insisted that she get rid of the baby because she was an intelligent woman who had been forgiven for the first baby. Another one would be unforgivable. And now that she was supposedly gay, she needed to try to sort some things out.

Even though she rarely saw Gayle, Chris had grown fond of her but relished in telling everyone else, "I can't stand that bitch."

Gayle had been over a couple of times and they had fucked, but Chris hadn't said a word about her pregnancy. Her eating habits changed almost immediately and didn't go unnoticed.

"You sure are putting away some food. You've eaten four catfish fillets tonight. And French fries. And rice. Usually you can barely eat just one piece of fish."

"Aren't you supposed to eat when you're pregnant?" Chris said sarcastically.

"Yeah, but you ain't pregnant." Gayle paused on her way to the kitchen and turned to her. "Chris, I know you ain't let me go up behind no man?"

Chris knew it was best that she didn't say shit.

"Chris?"

"Girl, it happened back when you was running up behind Marsha's ass. Didn't mean shit. I don't even talk to him anymore."

"Are you sure you're pregnant?"

"Nope. It's just a feeling I've got. Something you obviously don't know shit about."

"You don't know that," Gayle mumbled while clearing the table.

"What are you mumbling about?"

"Nothing. You had a test already?"

"I bought one to do later—once you take your ass home. It's in the bathroom," she said, gulping a longneck.

"Naw, you take that shit now." Gayle went to the bathroom and got the test out of the bag. "Here, and by the way, I only fuck with Marsha when you act like a damn fool. She understands that, and I wish you would, too. It's just a piece of ass."

"Uh-huh." Chris took the test into the bathroom and pissed on the strip. She didn't bother to read the instructions that said she was supposed to wait five minutes. Instead she left the test on the counter and went back into the kitchen to finish eating.

Ten minutes later Gayle went into the bathroom and looked at the test. After reading the instructions, she called Chris to the bathroom.

"Have you looked at this?"

"Nope."

"Well, here, Miss College Graduate. Take a look."

"You can barely see anything, Gayle. Throw it away." Chris turned to walk away.

"Chris, you aren't supposed to see anything if you ain't trying to be pregnant. This damn thing has changed colors!"

"Don't worry, I'm going to get rid of it first thing next week. When are you leaving anyway? I don't want any company."

Gayle left the room and began packing her belongings that had accumulated over the weeks. She couldn't stand an argument with Chris today. She had been let go from her temporary assignment and was in need of some comfort and companionship. She couldn't bear to tell her friends that she was out of another job, and she was too embarrassed to mention it to Chris because she knew that it would fall beneath Chris' high standards. But then she started thinking about what she felt when she was with Chris. Although her attitude was horrible, Gayle knew that Chris could be loved. She was the kind of woman that Gayle wanted to flaunt in front of her friends. She wasn't like the waitresses or the cashiers that she used to date. She had class and intelligence. She wanted to show them that, despite her history, she could nab the best of them. And finally here she was with a woman who had a college degree and a Howard degree at that. This was the opportunity of a lifetime. After she got her shit together, Chris would soon be bringing home some mega-dollars and would be able to give her the life that she always dreamed of. The house. The cars. The clothes.

DAMN!

She walked into the living room and saw Chris sprawled out on the floor listening to the stereo. Gayle took a seat next to her. "Look, I'm not going to let you shut me out. Don't get rid of the baby. It's not that child's fault that you and the pappy were irresponsible. God will never forgive you for that."

Chris looked at Gayle. "He won't forgive me for killing a baby, but He'll forgive me for bumpin' pussies with you?"

"No one sin is greater than the other, Chris."

"That's some shit, Gayle. I'm not even going to get into this with you. Get out," she said, walking to the front door.

"I ain't goin' no damn where. You're gonna listen to me."

Chris looked at Gayle and saw that she was trying to be serious. "What do you want from me? I treat you like shit. Put you out in the middle of the night."

"All of that let's me know that you love me, but you're afraid to let me know it."

"Do tell. I wouldn't count on all that."

"Keep the baby for me, Chris. If I have to work two jobs to pay the bills, I will. I care a lot about you and your crazy ass. I want you to quit working and spend your time concentrating on getting that baby here. Fuck the daddy. For what it's worth, I'm the daddy."

In her heart, Gayle wanted to make up for some other mistakes she had made in her life. Chris was completely stunned and let up a little bit, realizing that Gayle was going to want to move in permanently. After all Chris had done to push her away, Gayle still wanted to stay. Their sexual chemistry demanded that they be in the same house, in the same bed—all the time. Gayle understood that neediness, but Chris was in for the ride of her life.

Oblivious to the fact that she was making a deal with the devil and would never be able to afford to repay what she knew she'd ultimately owe, Chris dismissed the notion that she'd grown to not need anybody. "Well, just as long as you pay all the bills." Chris chuckled.

"All of them," Gayle agreed. "I'll pay all of them."

▲

Whenever the weather was nice, Gayle and Chris would get in the car and ride. They rode to Mississippi, to Missouri, and even to Arkansas, just to satisfy Chris' cravings for Hawaiian shaved ice from a little stand alongside a dirt road. It wasn't until she'd met Gayle that Chris knew that Overton Park was a popular hangout for ebony lesbians and gays in Memphis. On those exclusive Sunday afternoons, they would take Chelsea to the park for a picnic and to play at the playground. And their lovemaking? It was more passionate than either one of them had ever experienced.

Gayle felt the time was right for Chris to know about the daughter that she had given away when she was a teenager. Every time she got ready to tell her, though, something would come up. One night during their lovemaking, Chris noticed a dark, vertical line on Gayle's stomach—identical to the one she was redeveloping on her own. Chris then completely understood those maternal instincts that Gayle possessed. Respecting her privacy, she never questioned her about it. Chris' passion for Gayle began to heal some of the things that had haunted her. The pain of being a lesbian had begun to ease for her. Her relationship with Trey remained distant because she still felt that he had betrayed her.

10

Damage control was ignored when Trey decided that his relationship with Chris was over. Feeling that his transformation had been involuntary, he concluded that he wanted to undo what Chris had done to him. His cold and insensitive attitude toward Chris—toward the end of and after the relationship—was his way of rebelling against her and her actions. He did everything he could do to forget about her but, in the process, he had sacrificed his relationship with his daughter. Out of the clear blue sky, Trey decided that looking at other women wasn't such a bad thing. It was actually a pleasure. Later, he saw that there were still some things he didn't quite have a grip on…like his dick.

It only took one good fuck with a girl from a house party for Trey to forget about his baby and to forget about his relationship with Chris. This woman didn't bitch like Chris, nor did she act like Chris. Trey relished in her presence and in her youth. They were able to laugh and talk about things that he and Chris never could. It didn't even matter to him that this woman had another man's child and was desperately seeking a sucker—with a little cash in the bank—on the rebound. Darcy was a true friend to Trey, but she had a "girlfriend" obligation to Chris. So every little bit she knew, Darcy relayed it to Chris. Trey was deliberately telling his business to Darcy because he knew she was keeping an eye on him.

Problems between Chris and Gayle began when Trey started calling again. For some reason, he had become so pompous and standoff-ish since his separation from Chris. Although he had initially told Darcy to tell Chris that he needed time for himself, he started dating almost immediately, taking this free time to explore the life that he had been restricted from experiencing while he was with Chris. He went clubbing with his boys and readily increased the amount of female company that he kept. Trey found out about all of Chelsea's milestones through Darcy; the only link to his child. Though fully aware of his new girlfriends, Darcy never hesitated to remind Trey that he had a child with whom he desperately needed to establish a relationship. But as far as Trey was concerned, Chelsea was with the one woman that he wanted to stay as far away from as possible. It was a terrible price to pay, but that was the way it had to be. "To hell with Chris," was all that he ever had to say. Trey even went to Australia for vacation and never cared that he hadn't sent child support in months.

Chris couldn't handle Trey's attitude, and Gayle didn't want her talking to him because he always upset Chris so. With her pregnancy, Chris' attitude worsened, and Gayle did whatever she could to pacify her. One afternoon while Chris and Gayle were visiting Chris' mother, the phone rang. It was Trey returning a call from Chris—a call Gayle had known nothing about. After exchanging pleasantries with Trey, Ms. Desmereaux handed the phone to Chris.

"Trey, I simply asked you to send twenty dollars so I could get Chelsea some diapers. I never ask you for anything, but I need that money right now. I had to take off work to take care of Chelsea while she was sick."

"Well, I've got to buy tires. I'm not going another week without them. I'm sorry. There's snow and shit on the ground here, and I need 'em."

"Why are you taking this out on the baby? She hasn't done any-thing to you. You've had your ass all over the world, and you won't even send me twenty dollars?"

"I said that I have to buy tires, Chris. Good-bye."

Almost broke, Chris started crying and wiped her eyes before a single tear could fall. She had to, before Gayle spotted her. The slightest clue that she had been crying as the result of something that Trey had done or said would have meant a quick trip to D.C. to kick his ass. Gayle had become so protective of Chris that if it meant traveling almost a thousand miles to do it, then so be it.

To prevent upsetting her mother, Chris suggested that they leave. A furious Gayle couldn't wait to get back to the car.

As they drove toward home, Gayle asked, "Why the hell are you asking him for money? I told you we didn't need his money."

"He is her daddy, and she needs diapers. We have bills to pay, and the least he could do is buy her some damn diapers!"

Gayle glared at Chris. "Well, I'll tell you what. Since I pay the phone bill, I don't want his ass calling the house anymore. We can save the money from his collect calls and buy his baby some diapers!"

"Fuck you, Gayle." Chris threw Gayle's keys out of the window into a nearby field. She snarled at her. "Now you go find 'em."

Chris pulled over into a vacant parking lot, and Gayle got out. It took nearly an hour for her to find her keys. When she did find them, she kept walking down the street. Chris followed her in the car to a nearby pay phone, and watched her call every person she knew with a car. None of them were home.

Gayle finally said, "Take me home, Chris. I'm leaving."

They were nearly five miles from home, and knowing that Gayle would be pissed, Chris stopped by the mall.

"Chris, I want you to take me to the apartment so I can get my shit."

"Your ass can walk if you're in such a hurry. I've got something to do."

Before Chris could rise up out of the car seat, Gayle pushed her and punched her in the back.

"You're gonna take me home before you do anything. I'm sick of this."

Chris kept walking. Gayle followed her into Service Merchandise, scurrying to keep up with her. While waiting for the elevator, Gayle tried to talk to Chris, but she wasn't paying attention. When the elevator came, Gayle pushed Chris onto the elevator and started punching her. Chris got in one good lick before the elevator stopped. She didn't have any business at the mall. Chris was just being a bitch.

When they finally arrived at the apartment, Chris helped Gayle pack her things. "You can't stay here and hit on me. I can take almost anything—except that."

"Don't you think that you provoked me?"

"You aren't going to hit on me, if this is supposed to work."

"Girl, you've got some problems. You're just a crazy mutha-fucka!" Gayle said while packing the clothes basket that she used for luggage. Then, without any warning, Chris turned and spit on her. Gayle instinctively pushed her, and Chris hit the floor...flat on her stomach. "I hope I killed the bastard."

For almost ten minutes, Chris lay there crying. She didn't move. She couldn't move. The pain was so intense that she feared and sincerely hoped that Gayle had saved her a trip to the abortion clinic. After her last trip to the car, Gayle went back to the bedroom to find Chris still on the floor.

"C'mon, baby. Let me help you get up. I'm so sorry."

"I can't move. It hurts too bad."

"You want me to call an ambulance? You may need to get looked at."

"So I can tell them what when they get here? I was pushed?"

Chris was right. It wouldn't look good at all. Gayle helped her up and put her in the bed. She sat with her for hours, holding Chris in her arms. Before they fell asleep, they made passionate love.

"I'm sorry, Gayle," Chris whispered.

The next morning Chris helped Gayle empty the clothes basket and move her things back into their bedroom.

A week later Gayle got a job working for an office supply company. It was a temp-to-perm position right up her alley. She and Chris needed money. They needed it desperately. The rent was behind, and they were also trying to save money for the baby's arrival. Initially, she was hired as a data entry clerk but within weeks, her duties were expanded to include responsibilities in the purchasing department as well. The company sent her to Omaha for training, gave her a raise and her own desk. Antonie Moore, the warehouse manager, had been with the company for over five years. He was the only Black man who knew all the ins-and-outs of the purchasing department because everything in the warehouse was ordered through there. One morning he spotted Gayle coming in and offered to take her to lunch.

"There are some things we need to talk about," he said as they sat together at a table. "You sure are pretty, Miss Gayle." He smiled as he paid the cashier. She had wanted to go to Lotta Burger and, in spite of being a vegetarian, he took her anyway. "You married?"

Gayle just laughed. "No, I'm not."

"Got a boyfriend?"

She laughed again. "Kinda."

"What the hell kinda answer is that? Either you do or you don't."

"No, I wouldn't quite call it a boyfriend-girlfriend thing. We're kinda doin' our own thing. What you need to know for anyway?"

Gayle knew that her marital status had been the talk of the office. She always managed, however, to give her relationship with Chris some type of acknowledgment. "I'm seeing somebody and it's pretty heavy. And that's all you and yo' nosy ass coworkers need to know."

"Hey, hey, now, I was just asking. Who dat pretty ass girl that picks you up sometimes? She sho is fine! Damn!"

Beaming with pride, Gayle responded, "That's my sister, and don't even waste yo' time because she's taken. She's got a baby on the way anyhow."

Antonie laughed. "Hey, I can make her think twice about…"

"No, you can't," she said defensively. "She's committed to her relationship. I know that for a fact. Can we please change the subject? You didn't bring me out here to talk about my personal business. So wassup, niggah?"

Antonie took a look around him and rolled up his window. "Look here, baby girl, you wanna make some money?"

"What kinda money?"

"Well, that all depends on you. This is what you gotta do." Antonie told Gayle about a moneymaking scheme that would cure all of her financial woes. The possibilities would be endless—provided that everything was done correctly. "So you down or what, Gayle? You ain't got nothing to worry about. I'm gonna have yo' back if somebody says something. Aiight?"

Gayle knew that Chris would have a fit if she ever found out, but they needed the money. The most important thing to Gayle was to keep Trey away by any means necessary. Thinking about the love she and Chris had for each other, and all the things that she had wanted and needed to do for her, she replied with a simple nod of her head.

Just before Chelsea's first birthday party, Trey called and wanted to visit. Chris had never mentioned Gayle to him, nor had she mentioned that she was gay. The only way to protect her secret was to ask Gayle to leave until Trey had gone back to Maryland. Although she cared deeply for Gayle, she had no desire to completely exclude Trey from her life. If there was any opportunity for reconciliation, she wanted it. She consulted every friend she knew on how to win him back. Bubble baths, exquisite meals and special gifts were only some of the things that were suggested. Everything was perfect, until Gayle said that she wasn't leaving.

"Gayle, please, can you go back home until he leaves? He's only going to be here a couple of days."

"How can you ask me to leave my home? You asked me to come

here, and now you're asking me to leave for that fucka's benefit?"

"It's for the baby. He doesn't know that I'm gay, and he doesn't know that I'm pregnant. I want to use this time to tell him."

"I can't believe you, Chris."

Later that same afternoon, they rode to Waffle House to get something to eat. Chris felt that she was wrong for asking Gayle to leave, but it had to be done. There was no other way.

"I'll come to see you every night."

Gayle turned to Chris and, for the first time, Chris saw Gayle cry. "Don't worry about it. You don't have to. Just take me home so I can get my stuff."

"Baby, I wish that you would understand me."

"Chris, take me home to get my stuff."

After days of going back and forth with Trey, he ended up not coming. He sent Chelsea lots of gifts for her birthday but, because of the hateful feelings between him and Chris, he just could not bear the confrontation. Out of spite, Chris felt no better time than the present to tell Trey of her new lifestyle. She wanted to rub in his face that she had a woman who could do his job, in and out of bed, even better than him. And if that weren't enough, Chris longed to be there when his friends found out she had left him for a woman. But in actuality, Chris was despondent and disappointed. The only man who had consistently been there for her, without hesitation and without lies, did not want her anymore. To her, he possessed everything her father did not. That was all that she wanted from him. He was as transparent and as honest as she had ever known any man to be and, over the last months, she had watched her work crumble right before her eyes. When she did tell him about her lifestyle, his only comment about her new relationship was, "I only hope that you're serious about it."

One down. One to go. Telling him about the baby was next.

11

C hris was ready to pop by late September. She and Gayle had managed to make it through the summer, even though their fights were becoming more intense and more frequent. Making only $7.50 an hour, Gayle kept the rent paid and kept clothes on Chris' and Chelsea's backs. Monthly food stamps provided extra money and ample food, but Gayle's income alone was not enough to afford the weekly shopping sprees to Wal-Mart and the daily trips to lavish restaurants. Since all of her needs were being met, Chris didn't complain, but she did become concerned when the home computers started coming to their apartment and when Gayle had rolls of money in her pocket all the time. The only way that Chris could lash out was through violent, physical attacks on Gayle. Because of what had happened at the beginning of the pregnancy, Gayle vowed to never hit Chris while she was pregnant—no matter how vicious the attack.

With all the drama and frustration, there was no surprise when Chris' blood pressure elevated. Carrying close to eighty extra pounds, her doctor put her on bed rest for the remaining weeks of her pregnancy. While watching her car being repossessed, she went into premature labor one weekend while Gayle and Patty were away at a choir concert in St. Louis. It was then that she realized that Gayle hadn't been paying the bills as she had said. Granted, there was a lot of money floating around and, instead of taking care of priorities, Gayle had splurged. In the end, there was nothing to show for it but a lot bruises, pawn tickets, hurtful words and more unpaid bills.

The last week of October, Trey decided to take his trip to Memphis. Without any discussion, he called and announced his flight's arrival time for the next day. Chris' mother offered to pick him up from the airport, but Chris wanted to do it. When Chris greeted Trey at the airport, her belly got there first.

"What's this?" he said looking at Chris' waist.

"What does it look like?"

"Damn, are you due some time today?" he joked.

"No, a couple of weeks or so," she said as they walked to the car. Trey put his bags in the trunk and proceeded to open the driver's side door for Chris. "Don't worry about it. I can get it myself," she said.

"You forgot to tell me or something?"

"Nope." Her horns were beginning to show.

"Excuse me?"

"It really isn't any of your business, Trey. You've been doing your thang, and I've been doing mine."

"Obviously."

"I'm quite sure that you haven't been spanking little Jack Horner down there all by yourself. It's best that you just mind your business."

Trey was fuming. "Well, none of my money's going to take care of it!"

"You muthafucka! None of your money's been taking care of the one you got!" At this point, Chris was trembling. She knew that once they got back to her apartment, things weren't going to be much better. Gayle would be on a warpath. "Look, I'm not in any condition to go through this today. You can stay at my place, and I'll feed you. But I don't need the interrogation. You got it?"

Trey stubbornly stood there looking at her.

"YOU GOT IT!" she screamed.

"Yeah, I got it."

Confused about what he was feeling, Trey realized that Chris had moved on without an ounce of remorse or respect for him or his feelings.

That day nothing seemed to go right for Chris. Gayle called from the office and said that she was staying at a hotel. This brought Chris to tears, and she begged Gayle to come home.

"I'm not staying in that house with him. I'll bring you something to eat, but I'm not staying."

"Gayle, please, don't do this to me this week."

"I'll tell you what. I'll come get you, and you stay with me. Let him bond with his child."

"I can't do that. He doesn't know anything about taking care of her."

"Well, I've said all I have to say. The decision is yours."

Later that night, Gayle came home and found Chris sound asleep. She got into bed and reached around Chris' stomach. Kissing her shoulder and the nape of her neck, Gayle felt a damp spot in the bed. She pulled back the sheets and noticed that the bed was wet beneath Chris.

"Chris! Chris! Wake up!" she screamed. "Did you pee in the bed?"

During those last weeks, the baby had been putting a lot of pressure on Chris' bladder.

"What?" Chris asked incoherently.

Leading Chris' hand to the saturated sheets, Gayle said, "Feel this."

"Ewww!" Chris sighed. "That's not pee. Call my mother."

Ms. Desmereaux came as quickly as she could, and poor Trey had managed to sleep through the entire ordeal until Gayle walked by him and kicked him in the back.

"Damn," she said. "Ain't you good for anything? I'm taking Chris to the hospital. Her water broke. Her mother is in the back with Chelsea. Don't answer the phone or go to the door. You should have plenty of food in there."

Trey was still disoriented when he finally grasped what was going on. "Where is she?"

"Why? She ain't yo' concern no more." Then she turned and walked out the door. As she pulled the door shut, she laughed. "Oh, by the way, nice to meet you." And then she slammed the door.

Arriving at the hospital in the middle of a shift change was like walking into a subway station during rush hour. The nurses that were ending their shifts weren't assisting any patients because it was the end of their shifts, and the nurses beginning their shifts were too busy trying to get settled in. Therefore, once she was given a room, Chris and Gayle were pretty much on their own. By midnight, Gayle had rung for the nurse three times, and still no one had shown up.

"Don't ring it anymore, Gayle. They aren't going to come until they get ready to."

Chris was contracting more with this baby than she had with Chelsea and had not expected the labor to be so painful. When a nurse finally arrived, Chris was in the bathroom and announced that her mucous plug was coming out. The nurse paged the desk, and Chris was immediately taken to labor and delivery. Chris' regular obstetrician wasn't on call and, to complicate matters, the on-call doctor had three other babies making their debuts at the same time. He finally showed up during one of Chris' worst contractions. Afterwards, Dr. Jordan did a pelvic exam to see where the baby was located. To look at him, one would think that he was a rapper dressed in doctor's clothing. He had a medallion with the radius of a CD around his neck, dangling from a gold rope chain that looked like a piece of heavy rope that had been dipped in gold. Across his beautiful smile were three gold teeth that reflected light from the ceiling into Chris' face.

Drunk with pain medication, Chris snapped, "Who the hell are you?"

He really did look like a rapper getting ready to do a video about hospitals.

"Baby gurl." He grinned. "I'm Dr. Jordan, and it looks like we got a problem."

She could barely lift her head from the pillow when she started ranting and raving about his identity. Her speech slurred and vision blurred, Chris told him to get his hands off her because she wanted to wait for her own doctor.

Chris asked, "What do you mean, he's not here?"

Gayle took her hand, explaining that Dr. Jordan was just as good as her own doctor and that he was too busy to go back and forth with her.

"You're not dilating fast enough, and the baby is moving faster than you. So, to keep the baby out of danger and to give you some relief, I'm gonna have-ta cut ya. We're going to prep you for a C-section."

Dr. Jordan, who was notorious for teasing and scaring the hell out of his anesthetized patients, left the room and returned to check her again. Upon his two-fingered exam, he realized that she'd jumped from five centimeters to ten centimeters. Her contractions were less than a minute apart and, through all the pushing and the screams, Gayle was right there.

"Now, Chris, you're going to need to relax because the doctor's really busy tonight. Just breathe in and out for me," the nurse said calmly. Jessica was the same nurse that helped deliver Chelsea.

"How much longer?" Chris cried.

"That depends on this baby of yours. It's been trying to come here for the last several weeks. Now, all of a sudden, it's shy! You're ready, but I think it's gonna need a little help." She laughed.

Chris reached over to Gayle, who had been holding her hand the entire time. "You aren't gonna leave me here, are you?"

Looking straight into Chris' eyes, Gayle replied, "Why would I do that? I've been here all this time."

"Don't even think about trying it!" Chris squeezed her hand so tightly that her lover's fingertips were purple. "There's something that I need to tell you."

"Tell me while you're having a contraction. It'll help you concentrate." Gayle helped Chris breathe through the next three contractions. The baby's head had begun to crown. After two more pushes, Chris was told to stop, but the baby kept coming. Gayle's eyes glistened while watching the baby's formidable entrance into the world. Her heart was full and, for the first time, her life was purposeful. Unlike during the birth of her own child, Gayle's soul was in the room. The love that she felt for Chris had come full circle. "You can tell me now because there's nothing that you can say that will steal this moment away from me."

"I love you, Gayle."

Tears streamed from Gayle's eyes. It was the first time that Chris had ever said those words to her.

"Chris, honey, you've got a nine-pound six-ounce baby girl!" the nurse said.

Gayle walked over and proudly cut the umbilical cord.

As the nurse placed the pink bundle in her arms, Chris, with tears rolling down her face, smiled and said, "Hey, Gaylon Kirstain Desmereaux. Welcome, home."

Gayle stayed with Chris the entire time she was in the hospital. She had the most beautiful plant sent to her, a plant that represented a new beginning in their relationship. Patty even came to give his blessing and brought new clothes for the baby to wear home.

While they were leaving the hospital, Gayle looked at Chris, Chelsea, and Gaylon and said, "I've got a family. I really have a family."

Chris just smiled. "Yes, honey, you really do." They kissed each other and, even Gayle, with her inhibitions about publicly embracing a woman, didn't care who saw them.

▲

Gayle's mother, Sadie, and Chris had become exceptionally close during those nine months. On Sunday afternoons, dinner at Sadie's didn't start until Chris had arrived. Sadie seemed to be the link to Gayle's sometimes crude behavior since they were so much alike. She didn't speak much about it until one Sunday afternoon when Gayle had to sing at Mt. Canaan. Chris went along this time because, with one car, it was the only way that she was going to get to eat.

"Hey, Sadie! How ya doing, Sweet Sadie?" Chris always called her that.

"Fine, baby. How's my other daughter doing today?"

"We're hungry," Chris said, rubbing her stomach. "What did you cook? I hope you cooked some greens."

Sadie responded, "It's a surprise. I think you'll be pleased though." She touched Chris' belly. "Comin' right along, ain't you?"

"Don't remind me. I feel as big as a house. I can't even wear my church shoes anymore."

"Well, y'all leaving to go on over to the house when she finishes, right?"

"We're going to have to. This baby can't wait another minute to eat. We had a small lunch." Chris laughed. "And that isn't going to get it."

Sadie made sure that Chris was seated comfortably at the end of the pew and handed her a program. "Is this the first time you've ever heard her sing?"

"Uh-huh."

"I see. Well, I think she'll make you proud. She has a way of getting to people with her singing. I guess that's why she never talks much. You know, has she ever told you why we ain't that close?"

"No, she hasn't but, then again, there's a lot she doesn't tell me. She always seems to think that the whole world is against her. I do what I can for her, but it never seems to be enough."

"Has she ever told you about her little girl?"

Chris turned and looked Sadie straight in the eyes. "What?"

"She had a baby the January before she started school, and it was a little girl. She didn't want to have anything to do with her because she'd just gotten into this thing that y'all do and didn't want to be bothered. She said that a baby would tie her down, so she chose to give it away."

"Where's the baby now?"

"She's with that girl."

"What girl?"

"Sheila. You know anything about her?"

"A little. Gayle has mentioned her a couple of times. She never really goes into much detail about her. I only know that she's the sister of this guy named Roosevelt that used to like Gayle. Sadie, you know she tells me only what she wants me to know."

"Roosevelt loved that girl, and Gayle was too stupid to see it. After the baby was born, she said that she didn't want the baby anywhere near her, so Sheila took my only grandchild and left. Chris, I was so pissed, I mean—'scuse me, Lord—upset with her. That was my first grandchild. I think that Gayle was trying to get back at me for giving her to my sister."

"Who? Sara? You gave her to Sara?"

Sadie grabbed Chris' hand and squeezed it tight. "At the time, Gayle loved going to Sara's. She gave her everything that I couldn't, and Gayle loved her to death. I spent long hours at work and barely had time for myself—let alone Gayle. Sara gave her the attention that I couldn't. So I signed papers to let her stay over there. Then a few years later, I had another baby, and Gayle became very distant with me. I guess she felt that I didn't love her and didn't want her. Actually, I really did, but they'd become so attached to each other that it just didn't seem right to interfere."

"Have you ever tried to talk to Gayle about what you were really feeling back then?"

"Nah, I don't think that she really cares now. Besides, after Sara took sick, Gayle started losing her damn mind. Started doing crazy shit. 'Scuse me again, Lord," she said, looking to the sky. "But it's the truth. She stayed in trouble. She was always trying to get stuff the easy way. I imagine that was entirely Sara's fault because all Gayle had to do was ask for something and she got it."

Chris sat puzzled. "Are you sure that Gayle gave the baby up for that reason? That doesn't sound like her. She's been so helpful with this baby."

"Don't get me wrong, now. She just might have a good heart inside of that icebox of a body of hers. Her intentions are always good, but her judgment isn't always the best. Constantly thinking that the world owes her something. Since you've been coming around, I see that there's a lot that you don't know about her. I just want you to be careful. You don't seem to be like the folks she tends to run with."

"Sweet Sadie, can I ask you something?"

"Sure, baby, anything."

"How am I supposed to love her?"

"Carefully, baby. Very carefully. You do need to know this, though."

"What's that?"

"I didn't give her away, baby. I only wanted her to be happy. When my play brother and his son moved in with Sara to help out around the house, Gayle asked to come back home. 'Cause of my other kids, I told her no."

"You talkin' about Bo and Junior?"

"Yeah, Bo grew up with us. Our parents were good friends, and we just kinda looked after one another all the time. He and Junior left, about the same time we found out Gayle was pregnant. After that happened, we saw very little of Gayle. She stayed around Sheila a lot. We thought that maybe it was because she was the baby's auntie. Turned out it was more to it than that."

"Yeah, she told me about that." Chris' leg started trembling. "Ooh-wee!"

"What's wrong? You..."

"I have to pee real bad. Is she next?"

Sadie looked at the program. She and Chris had been whispering in the back of the church for nearly half the service. "She's after the announcements. You should make it back before then. Hell, if not, they've got speakers in there. Go on and handle your business."

"Okay. I really can't wait. Be right back."

As she got up from the pew, Sadie grabbed her hand. "Do you know what it is yet?"

Chris smiled at Sadie, leaned over and whispered in her ear, "It's a girl." Then she quickly wobbled to the bathroom to handle her business. Needless to say, she missed seeing Gayle's solo, but she heard every soothing note as her powerful voice carried over the loudspeaker in the bathroom.

▲

Minutes after Chris was released from the hospital, Gayle got a page from Sadie asking her to bring Chris and Gaylon over to her house. The relationship between Sadie and Gayle had somewhat strengthened since Chris started coming around. They saw each other more often, and they tried to talk at least twice during the week. Sadie noticed a change in her daughter. She was more subdued and had become more responsible. Still, there were secrets that Gayle kept deeply hidden.

"Bring that baby on in here!" Sadie yelled. When she saw Chris get out of the car after Gayle had taken the baby out of the back seat, she noticed that not only was Chris limping, but she also didn't have a thing covering her head. "Girl, you ain't got nothing on yo' head!" She slammed the door and ran to the back of the house.

Chris slowly made it to the front door. When she got ready to sit down, she noticed that her ankles and feet were swelling. Chris grabbed Gayle by her jacket. "What are we doing here? I need to..."

"Your in-laws wanted to see you." Gayle laughed. "We're only going to be here for a minute."

"All right."

The next things Chris saw were a bundle of balloons and a huge teddy bear. "I wanted to get you a little something for the baby," Sadie cried out. "And you know you always have a baby sitter."

"Thank you, Sweet Sadie. This is so sweet of you."

Even Gayle was shocked because never before had her mother taken such an interest in one of her lovers.

"And I found this in the back for you to put on your head when you go back out," Sadie added. "Yo' ass has been wide open, and you ain't got on a coat or nothing."

"Well, I thought we were going straight home, so I didn't even worry about it. I don't mean to rush off or anything, but I really need to get on home."

"I understand. It was good seeing you," Sadie said, reaching over and kissing Chris and Gaylon on their cheeks.

Gayle was beaming with pride and took her women home where the nursery had been decorated with Winnie the Pooh.

Chris was shocked. "How did you do this? You've been with me the whole time."

Blushing, Gayle said, "It comes in handy to have a bunch of queens for friends."

Gayle knew that they'd probably never show their faces around there again. Despite the baby's arrival, they still couldn't stand Chris. Their feelings, however, didn't matter to Gayle. She was in love with Chris. If Chris needed something, Gayle didn't waste a second getting it for her. Even in the middle of the night, Gayle got up and fed the baby and put her in the bed between them. She bought all of Gaylon's clothes and diapers. For the longest time, Chris didn't even know what size her own child wore. Gayle eventually began getting both girls up and dressed them, so that their mother could get some extra sleep. She took on all of the maternal responsibilities, and the few people that knew of her past were truly impressed. No one would have ever guessed that Gayle had a child of her own.

Gayle was fired from the very first job that she had because she got caught letting her friend, Sheila, take merchandise out of the store. At the next one she was let go because her cash drawer came up short every night. She had stolen credit card numbers from several customer receipts and found a gold mine full of opportunity. That gold mine turned to soot when she got caught by the police and ended up with probation. Then hardly three years later, she got into even more trouble, but this time she was living in Tulsa.

Her lover at the time was Denise, who was not the most attractive girl. She was, however, madly in love with Gayle. Because her clerical skills were excellent, Gayle kept a job with a temporary service and landed an opportunity of a lifetime. They asked her to relocate to Tulsa because Ford Motor Credit was opening a new customer service center. She had just started dating Denise, but their relationship was pretty heavy. Gayle was Denise's first, and whatever it took to keep the fire burning, Denise did. So, she went with her.

Denise found out shortly after she arrived that she was five months pregnant. Realizing that it had happened long before she had come along, Gayle offered to take care of her while she was pregnant. Soon, however, money began to run short, and there was nothing that Denise could do at eight months pregnant. So Gayle gave Denise her checkbook and let her write checks against her bank account. Then they reported them stolen. Everything they bought, or stole, was sold for money to pay the bills. They were caught and prosecuted. Denise, with a new baby boy, was granted immunity for testifying against Gayle. Gayle was given two years probation.

After that there was obvious tension and unhappiness. The attention that Denise had once given to Gayle was now being given to Justin, and there was no way that Gayle could compete with that. It was then that she vowed to never date a woman with children. It took away from the relationship and brought more problems than a few.

One afternoon, in a fit of frustration, she slapped Justin in the face. When Denise confronted her about it, she snapped, "Why the hell would I hit a nine-month-old baby?" If it had not been for the swollen handprint on his face, Denise would have been content believing that Gayle never meant him any harm.

▲

A week later, Gayle lost her job and asked Denise to try and get some assistance. She was given almost $300 a month in cash and $450 in food stamps. Then suddenly, Gayle started dating this guy named Stephan. They started fucking within a matter of days, and she spent more and more time away from home, showing up around the first of the month when the check came in. Once it was gone, she disappeared, too.

Stephan fell in love with Gayle and wanted to get married. Instead of dignifying his proposal with a response, Gayle told Denise that she was ready to move back to Memphis and that she didn't have time to wait for her to get her things together. She was ready to go right then. Violating her probation, Gayle left and, without an ounce of remorse, she left Denise and her son behind to fend for themselves.

For Denise revenge was all too sweet. She called Gayle's probation officer and turned her in. She also called the company that had financed Gayle's car and told them where she was and, when Gayle returned to Tulsa to answer for her probation violation, her car was repossessed while she was at the courthouse. She tried to call Denise, but the phone had been disconnected. Denise, unbeknownst to Gayle, was headed back to Memphis in a rental car.

Shortly before Gayle moved to Tulsa, Aunt Sara had suffered a massive heart attack that was later complicated by a severe stroke that had left her paralyzed. Against all odds and to the doctor's surprise, Aunt Sara managed to live. Too many days and nights passed with her cursing God for not allowing her to die. She didn't want rehab or anything to help her get better. The family united and helped out as best they could. That was the story Gayle gave her probation officer when she was questioned about leaving town. Needless to say, he fell for it, and he arranged for her to return to Memphis—provided that she paid her fees and sent in monthly reports. Once she got back to Memphis, she never did either.

Having convinced Sadie that she would help care for Sara, Gayle got a bus ticket home, and, instead of sticking to her promise, moved in with Renee—a member of the Greater Community Workshop Choir. After attending several of the group's concerts and rehearsals, they asked her to join them. Her solos put the choir on the map and, within a matter of months, she was back in business with her singing career. Living with Renee exposed Gayle to the other side of the gospel choir circuit.

They smoked dope and drank just like everybody else. Hell, sometimes they even performed better when they were high. Another thing she noticed was that mostly everybody was gay. They passed each other around like roaches and relished in discussing their escapades with one another. They would go to concerts and sing until they brought the house down; leave there and go straight to the club; come home and fuck until the sun came up; and, if that morning were a Sunday, they went to church. The guilty ones were always the best singers and were also the ones who "performed" in the aisles on Sundays.

Renee and Gayle kicked it for a while. Gayle got a job working for Federal Express and was making enough money to send Renee roses every other day. Avoiding commitment, Renee dated Gayle and a couple of other people. Gayle eventually got tired of being used by Renee because all of the money Gayle gave her was spent to get high. So she moved on and went back to Sara's.

The temporary service that had sent her to Federal Express found out about her criminal record and terminated her employment without notice. Gayle, whose skills ranked among the elite in the clerical pool—thanks to her 85 wpm and fine-tuned computer capabilities—had another assignment, with another temporary service, within a matter of days. Work began almost immediately. She wasn't guaranteed an assignment every day, so she wasn't guaranteed a paycheck every week. Most of her free time was spent with Patty, Dexter, and the rest of the crew. Everybody had an agenda except her. Whenever she got hold of a stolen credit card, she bought new clothes and treated her buddies to shopping sprees. She didn't care what the repercussions would be if she got caught. She didn't think about what would happen if her friends ditched her when she needed them most. Besides, most of her friends knew the credit card and check scams like the back of their hands, and many of them knew when to stop. Those that didn't stop had the misdemeanors and felonies on their records that would follow them forever and would also prevent them from ever getting decent jobs. Finding a sugar daddy or sugar momma was the only means of survival and, if they got into a financial bind, there were always the checks and the credit cards. The vicious cycle continued from one generation to another. Always trying to get something for nothing.

▲

Every Wednesday after work Gayle picked up a copy of the *Memphis Flyer*. She started scanning the personals for women. The first woman she met was named Beverly, and all she really wanted was someone to fuck her while her boyfriend watched. She and Gayle performed for him a number of times and, once, she'd even done Beverly and a friend of hers at the same time. After that one there were many more. That is until she answered Chris' ad.

Each ad in the *Flyer* was given a voice mailbox for responses. Gayle left a message for Chris, but it was almost two days before she received a reply. Intrigued by Chris' voice and her apparent intellect, Gayle called Dexter and asked him to ride with her to the other side of town.

"You going where?"

"I wanna go over here and check out this girl I met. I wanna see if the face matches the voice."

"You oughta be tired of meeting women like this. You don't meet people in the newspaper." He hesitated for a minute. He had to admit that it would be nice to see one of them in person. Up until then, he had only heard about them. "I'll go with you, only if we can stop by and pick up Chante. She's got something to talk to me about and the damn phone is off. She can tell me while you're in there hoing around."

Gayle said, "I'll be there in a couple of minutes."

She had gotten a little hoopty for a couple of hundred dollars. It sputtered and shit, but it got her where she needed to go. It took her almost half an hour to get to Chris' house. Though it was dark out, they could still see the big houses and nice cars along Chris' street. When Gayle found her house, she chuckled to Dexter. "If I'm longer than five minutes, come in and get me."

"Hell, I wanna get out and see this muthafucka myself!"

"Don't act so ghetto, Dexter. Sit yo' punk ass in here and talk to yo' buddy."

Chante and Gayle were not the best of friends but, if her coming along was the only way that Dexter was going to accompany her, then she had to put up with her.

Gayle rang the doorbell. When Chris answered, Gayle knew that the woman that now stood in front of her was definitely the one. This girl doesn't do checks and credit cards, Gayle thought to herself. She had the fairest of complexions without a blemish on her face. Her hands glided gracefully as she moved things around on the sofa so her guest could sit down.

"Oh, I'm not going to stay. I just wanted to stop by for a minute," Gayle said.

Chris excused herself and came back with a baby carrier with a baby in it.

"Ooh, how pretty! Whose baby is this?"

"Mine."

Damn, she's got kids, Gayle thought.

Disappointed, Gayle hurriedly motioned toward the door and told Chris that she'd call her later.

"Well, what's she like? She looks pretty," Dexter commented.

"She's cute. Kinda fat, though."

"Well, that's cool, ain't it?"

"Yeah, but that bitch got a baby. She ain't said shit about that before."

"Oh, well, baby, better luck next time," he joked. "Let's make this damn journey back across town."

By the time she'd dropped them off at home, Gayle had realized, for the sake of something new, that a baby might not be all that bad. Gayle quickly recognized that this woman was seemingly flawless. In order to enter and stay in this woman's world, Gayle surmised she could never tell Chris of her criminal past or of her unstable employment history.

12

"How in the hell can you go to church on Sunday mornings and minister to a congregation of nearly one thousand people when you just got out of bed with a woman?"

Chris' question from that brisk, Sunday morning had burned a hole into Gayle's conscience. In all their months together, they had overcome many problems. Chris had been there for her when the rest of the world had not. Gayle had been appointed the Minister of Music in a church where it was etched in stone that a woman's place was in the kitchen of the church as cooks, in the pews of the church as members of the Mother Board, and in the aisles of the church as ushers. Chris had written a letter of application to help Gayle, who had yet to take a single class, get into college, and probably, most importantly, Chris had helped her with her legal problems by getting her the best lawyers to keep her out of jail for things that she had done to help make ends meet. Gayle had never bothered to tell Chris anything about her or her past. She only mentioned those things that would put them on the same level.

Gayle was a smooth and talented singer. In high school, she could sing anything you put in front of her, any range, and any genre. She was not only the class valedictorian her senior year but also the First Chair Alto in the all-city and all-state choirs. The bitch was bad. College scholarships beckoned from all areas of Tennessee for both music and academics.

The night of her senior prom Gayle and Roosevelt, brother of Sheila—the prettiest and sexiest girl in the junior class—took pictures at his mother's house before going to his father's house to do the same thing. Sheila lived with her father during the week but, since it was her big brother's prom night, her Friday night excursion across town to her mother's was delayed. She wanted to see her brother and his date and wish them well on their big night out.

Gayle had known Sheila from choir class where Sheila had been Mrs. Benedict's fifth-period aide. She had accompanied the choir on all of its engagements and, for the guys, she provided the nicest of views on the hottest of school days—especially when attired in halter-tops and tight jeans. Thanks to her height and lean, svelte body, all of the girls envied her. To top it off, she was smart as a whip as well as gorgeous. You would have thought that a hand over the crotch was the school symbol since none of the boys wanted to get caught in their wet daydreams about her. Though Sheila basically talked to no one, she found a soothing comfort in Gayle's presence. When passing out sheet music, Sheila always picked the songs that Gayle led and would just sit and stare into her eyes, never chancing to miss hearing or feeling a note. It seemed that she was absorbed in a secret that only she and Gayle shared.

Sheila didn't have on her usual tight bell-bottoms and sneakers when Gayle and Roosevelt arrived at his father's house. Instead, she donned a pair of tight denim daisy dukes that defiantly hugged the lips of her coochie with a white knit T-shirt that embraced every curve of her breasts. Her smooth, long legs glistened from the top of her coffee-colored thighs to the tip of her freshly polished toes. Wet from shampooing, her hair was sandy brown accented with blonde streaks. Each natural curl dangled in the middle of her back. The water spot on the front of her T-shirt gave Gayle an easy and pleasurable view of her protruding nipples. The cool breeze from the ceiling fan only enhanced the effect. In school, Gayle's only sight of Sheila was with a ponytail that was always pinned to one side of her head. Closing her eyes for only a brief second, Gayle was mesmerized by the view. Bouncing down the stairs, Sheila actually looked much like a gutter rat hoe. But to Gayle, she was the most beautiful woman she had ever seen.

Though she stood still, Gayle's mind was racing. Fuck the prom. This is my night, she thought. I want to take off this $300 satin gown and put on a pair of hot pants, too. Where all of this was coming from Gayle did not know, but the secret that she and Sheila shared was about to be revealed.

"Y'all know y'all sharp!" Sheila giggled. She had the prettiest smile, flashing perfect teeth. "Wish I could go," she said shyly.

"Girl, you got next year. Ain't nobody gonna be there but a bunch of niggahs trying to get some pussy. Ain't that right, Gayle?" Roosevelt chuckled, nudging Gayle. He was definitely handsome but, compared to his sister, Roosevelt wasn't shit.

"Don't get your hopes up, chile. We ain't even ate yet," Gayle joked.

All of the excitement that most girls get on their prom night hadn't even crossed Gayle's mind. After having seen Sheila, fucking Roosevelt was the last thing on her agenda that evening.

"Oh, I'm getting some of this ass," Roosevelt said as he grinned and pulled Gayle toward the door. "Ain't no doubt about that!"

"Whatever." Gayle sighed. "Whatever."

Roosevelt's father had gotten his son a room at the exclusive Peabody Hotel, site of their senior prom. Caught up in the excitement, he had not noticed that Gayle was a nervous wreck. She hadn't danced the whole evening and, despite her usual pleasant smile, she had barely cracked a grin in the pictures. Dozens of girls would have killed to go to the prom with Roosevelt Harper, the finest guy in the senior class. He had won every senior superlative category that he was nominated for and had been heavily recruited by several Ivy League schools. Instead, his choice had been the Marines. And, on this night, his special night to remember, he was spending the evening with a girl who only had thoughts of his sister.

▲

"Girl, what's wrong with you? You've been quiet all evening. Did I do something to offend you? You act like you don't want me to touch you."

"I'm aiight, Roosevelt. I just got tired of watching all those bitches tuggin' on you all night. Wantin' a kiss. Wantin' to take pictures. Shit, they might as well have taken you out back and fucked you in the alley. Women will never change. Always throwin' themselves at some man."

Reaching for her hand, he said, "Baby, I chose you to go to the prom with."

Gayle smirked. "Yeah, just so that you could get some pussy."

"It ain't that, Gayle. I can get pussy anytime, anywhere. I really do like you, and I have for a long time. You fine. You smart. If I wasn't going off to the Marines, I would…"

"Wait a minute, Roosevelt, before you say anything else. We've had fun tonight. Let's not spend the night talking about a bunch of ifs and shit. I just want us to enjoy the rest of the evening."

She wistfully gazed out of the window at the Mississippi River as it calmly flowed past the banks of Tom Lee Park. Gayle was thinking about Sheila and those daisy dukes.

"But Gayle, would you please just listen to me. I think that we got something special. You so pretty, and, damn, you can sang!"

"Stop, Roosevelt."

"Please, baby." He started pulling her to him, but she kept pulling away. "Why won't you listen to me? I want to be with you. My dad got us this room, and I did all these beautiful things for you. Sheila told me to…"

The mere mention of Sheila's name brought warmth to Gayle and erased the boredom in her eyes.

"She told you what?" she asked softly. For the first time since they had been in the hotel room, Gayle looked deeply at Roosevelt. "She told you what, Roosevelt?"

"She told me some of the things that you might like."

"How could she do that? She doesn't even know me. We've never said more than two or three words to each other."

"Baby, she's a woman, and she oughta know what it takes to please one."

"I guess you're right," she responded. "Let's take a walk through the lobby. I've never seen the ducks. I need to get some air before this evening draws to a close. We can talk about all this other stuff later, okay?"

She was trying to do everything possible to keep from being alone with Roosevelt longer than she had to be.

Roosevelt grinned at Gayle. "Okay, but after this, it's on."

"Aiight."

The ducks in the lobby didn't impress Gayle nor did the concierge that escorted them back to their suite. Neither did the silk sheets nor the bottle of champagne that was placed next to the bed. Roosevelt had done his best to capture her attention and affection that night. He massaged her shoulders with body oil to try to relieve her tension. He poured her a glass of champagne and sat it next to the bed to quench her thirst. Before he undressed her, he even sprinkled rose petals from his boutonnière on the bed. He slowly draped his arms around her, gently pressing his toned, muscular body against hers. Gayle never even twitched when he entered her, for her mind was far away in another space—her thoughts caressing the memory of another face. His kisses she never returned. It was not his but someone else's kisses she desired. She only thought of kissing and making love to Sheila. So she closed her eyes and dreamed.

▲

It was after seven o'clock the next morning when Gayle finally got home. Her uncle and cousin greeted her at the door. Sara had left an hour earlier for work at the hospital. Because of her aunt's schedule, Gayle was at home alone most of the time.

"Looking pretty good there, Gayle. Say-ra waited on you, but she had to go on and get outta here. How was the prom?" Bo asked.

"It was fine." She was trying to get past them, but they kept blocking the doorway. Liquor on their breath never got a chance to get stale because they drank around the clock. They smelled so bad that Gayle did all she could to keep from puking.

"Why you in such a hurry?" Junior asked, balancing the butt of a cigarette between his lips. "We just want to look at ya in yo' pretty clothes."

"Will you please let me by? I need to get ready for church. Excuse me, please," Gayle demanded. She noticed that they were both drunk and shit just didn't seem right. "Move, dammit!" She pushed them out of her way.

"Go on then, bitch! Take yo' stuck up ass on!" Bo yelled as he and his drunken ass son went to the back of the house.

The water was way too hot, but Gayle didn't care. She wanted to wash off every memory of her prom night. As she lathered her skin, she massaged her breasts and thought of Sheila. She touched herself and enjoyed it. Then there was a knock at the door.

"Gayle!" a woman's voice shouted through the door. It was Sadie.

"Yeah?" she answered.

"How was the prom? I heard you looked real nice."

"I had a good time. We took some pictures and stuff. Went to dinner. You know typical prom stuff."

"Did you mess your dress up?"

"Naw, it's just a little wrinkled."

"Good. We can take it back tomorrow. You coming to church?"

Gayle went ahead and got out of the tub, since she obviously could not have any peace. "I'm coming. I'll be ready in about half an hour."

"Well, I just came by here to bring some greens for dinner this evening. I left my Bible at home, so I need to get back over there. Do you need a ride?"

"Yeah, I do."

"Well, I'll be back in a few."

"Okay. I'll be ready."

With the exception of Gayle, Bo, and Junior, the house was now empty.

Beads of sweat ran from Gayle's face as she left the bathroom. She ran straight for the air conditioner unit in the window and stood there as the blast of cold air dried her face. As soon as she turned her back to head for her room, she was pushed to the floor. Her face was slammed against the carpet so hard that her nose seemed to explode. A penis was rammed into her from behind with a force so strong that it tore the opening of her vagina. She fought to get up but was pinned down throughout the entire ordeal. Just as she thought it was over…just as she heard him gasp for air, another penis thrust into her.

"C'mon, bitch. What you gotta say now!"

This time, however, whoever it was had the mercy to flip her into the missionary position. Focusing through the tears, Gayle fixed her eyes on Bo who was comfortably inside of her. He'd covered her mouth with the sweaty palm of one of his big, dirty hands and tightly held her wrists together with the other. Bo withdrew before ejaculating, shooting a stream of steaming semen across Gayle's chest and face. And then, as suddenly as it had begun, the violation was over. No hands holding her wrists; no one gasping for air; no vile words; nothing but the smell of stale liquor and cigarette smoke. In the silence, Gayle realized that they had left her there as she heard the squeaky metal screen door slam against its wooden frame.

Sadie's horn blasted into Gayle's bedroom window. She was ready, except for the blood that she had to clean up in the hallway. She got a wet towel soaked in bleach and wiped down the entire floor. There was nothing she could do about the smell of stale alcohol in the house. She knew that Sara would take care of that when she got home. The aroma of collard greens, candied yams, asparagus casserole, fried chicken, and cornbread would fill the air, and the incidents of that morning would be long forgotten. The tear between her legs, although uncomfortably painful, was smeared with Neosporin and covered with a sanitary pad. The stinging sensation would disappear after urinating a few times. Trying her best not to limp, Gayle moved slowly toward her mother's car. Sadie had that "I'm on my way to church" smile on her face, and it seemed that she hadn't a care in the world. Instead of telling her mother what had happened, Gayle just carefully slid in the passenger's seat and took a long deep breath. All she wanted to do was to get out of that house.

"Mama?" she whispered. Not accustomed to being addressed as "Mama" by Gayle, Sadie did not answer. More intensely, she queried, "Mama?"

Then Sadie looked over at her daughter and saw that Gayle was looking directly at her. "You call me?"

"Yeah, I was thinking. I would like to come home to live with you. I mean, just for a little while. Maybe until Bo and Junior leave."

As she turned into the church parking lot, Sadie responded, "I don't think that would be a good idea. It's already five of us at my place. Besides, Sara would have a hissy fit if you left her. It's best to leave things like they are."

"But…"

"C'mon, honey, we runnin' late!"

Sadie never said another word about it.

Gayle made it just in time to march in with the choir. By now she couldn't help limping, and it took everything in her to keep from crying. The only thing on her mind was the touch of a woman... any woman...that would erase the filth that had embedded itself within her body, her mind, and her soul. Though she desperately longed for Sheila, Gayle knew her lustful wishes were wrong. However, she had been so betrayed by men that she refused to think otherwise.

It was on this Sunday that Reverend Mickens took his text from the Book of Romans—the first chapter. During the invitation, something came over Gayle. There was a burning inside of her that she had never known. The fire spread from her heart to the tips of her toes, and she raced down the aisle. With an overwhelming desire to praise God, Gayle belted out the most heartfelt "docta-wat" that anyone had ever heard. It brought every member of the congregation to his feet, and, one by one, they fell to their knees. Gayle was trying to say something, shame wouldn't allow her to speak. Afterwards she broke into a rendition of "God's Amazing Grace" and shook the church from the floor to the rafters.

Within the past twenty-four hours, Gayle's soul had accumulated secrets too shameful to repeat and too powerful to keep to herself. God, His sanctuary, and those who openly praised Him became her only friends.

13

Two months after the prom, Gayle was in Megamarket buying some Tums for her recurring indigestion. She had developed an unusual taste for red smoked sausages and strawberry milk. As she approached the dairy section to get a gallon of milk, someone touched her from behind.

· "Girllll, what you been doing? I ain't seen you since Ro-Ro's prom night!" a familiar voice exclaimed. "Where you been?"

Gayle turned around and looked into the eyes of the star of all her dreams. Sheila looked better than she ever had, and Gayle was determined not to let her get away this time.

"Hey, Chile! What's up?" Gayle asked, reaching for Sheila to give her a hug.

The smell of Halston perfume lingered heavily around her neck and, as she embraced Gayle, it seemed as if time stood still.

Slowly pulling away, she stroked the back of Gayle's head. "Your hair is still so pretty."

Gayle's heart began to flutter with that same feeling she had on her prom night when she saw Sheila in those daisy dukes. She realized, at that moment, that if she had been given the choice, a life with a man—not a woman—would have been inevitable. But this was the choice that someone else made for her. Many nights had passed when she couldn't sleep and days when she couldn't eat. She even sought solace in reading every page of the Bible, hoping for a miraculous cure. How could she discuss this embarrassing situation with anyone? All of the frustration and anguish was bubbling over, crying out for release. She had told no one of the morning after her prom, and she never planned to. Maybe that had been God's way of punishing her for lusting after a woman. There could be no other reason for that kind of hell. She had to deal with the demons haunting her. And she repented by being at every function and at every service every time the church doors opened.

Gayle tugged on her own hair. "Girl, this stuff is giving me fits! I've been wanting to cut it, but I think that I'm going to wait until I start school in the winter."

"Why you waiting until the winter?"

"I was late getting my shit in, and one of my scholarships doesn't fund until then." Gayle was not going to miss this opportunity to be alone with Sheila. If there was not an opening, she was going to create one. "How's your brother?"

"He's fine. Getting ready to leave for the service. He always asks me if I've heard from you and, of course, I hadn't until today. I can't wait to tell him that I saw you."

You ain't gotta, Gayle was thinking to herself. Her brain was smoking. She had to figure out how to get Sheila to come to her house. "Hey, look, I was about to go home and fix me some smoked sausages and strawberry milk."

"What?" Sheila laughed. "Smoked sausages and what?"

"Strawberry milk. Lately, I've had this thing for that stuff." Gayle grabbed a box of Crackerjacks and started eating them. She was famished. "You want to come over to the house for a drink or something? I know you're still under age and all." She laughed.

"Yeah, right. What you drinking?"

"Don't matter. Depends on what my cump-nee wants."

Sheila walked over to Gayle and put her arm around Gayle's shoulders. Gayle damn near fainted. Sheila leaned over and whispered in her ear, "Don't tell nobody, but I'm a Champale woman myself."

"Well, I tell you what. I'll take care of the licka, and you meet me at my house in an hour."

One of Gayle's church members was working the register up front, so she didn't have to worry about being carded. He owed her one anyway, for the five dollars she'd lent him some two years before. On Fridays, Sara had to work a double shift at the hospital, so Gayle had the place to herself. Her uncle and cousin had been in Detroit since May, and she hoped that their asses never came back. Having her aunt to herself was the most important thing to Gayle. When she was seven years old, Sadie asked her sister Sara to let Gayle come and live with her since Gayle was Sara's favorite niece, and she loved her as the daughter she never had. She and Gayle, from that point on, had been inseparable. Sara was working overtime to make sure that Gayle had everything that she needed for college, even if it meant working double shifts at the hospital.

Instead of cooking the smoked sausages, Gayle decided to create a meal. She pulled out her aunt's recipe book and whipped up an Italian dish called manicotti. It was the first time that she had ever tasted it, and it seemed far better than the original plan of smoked sausages and strawberry milk. Because Sara was a stickler for cleanliness, the house was always kept spotless and, to create a little romance on this evening, Gayle picked some fresh roses out of Sara's flowerbed. Just in case of the unexpected, Gayle put fresh sheets on her bed and lit candles throughout the house. She was as busy as a cat covering up shit while she was making preparations. Finally, she popped a slow jam tape into the stereo. Months before, she had made that tape with Sheila in mind.

Most doorbells in North Memphis didn't work, so Sheila didn't even bother. She knocked loudly enough to be heard over the radio. Gayle's rounded silhouette emerged from the kitchen. She unhooked the screen door and welcomed Sheila in.

As her ears caught the faint mellow grooves of Switch singing "There'll Never Be" Sheila squealed with delight. "Damn, girl.

You jammin', ain't you? Oo-oo-wee! I love this song...for the first time, you and I. Show me what you..." she sang. "Turn that up!" She giggled as she bounced and swayed through the doorway. But Gayle knew the words and, before this night was over, she was determined to sing them, especially for Sheila. Suddenly Sheila's nose caught the scent of a delectable aroma drifting around the dining room. "What smells so good in here? Sure as hell ain't no smoked sausages!"

"You're so silly. I decided to cook something else," Gayle responded. "Can't invite somebody over to your house for some damn hot dogs on a Friday like this. Want something to drink?"

"Naw, I ain't drinking on no empty stomach. Can't be held responsible for what I might do," Sheila said coyly.

Even on a mid-July night such as this one, the temperature hovered at 90 degrees. Sheila had on a tank top and some shorts. She had cut her hair to just above her shoulders, but she was still gorgeous. Nothing could change that fact. Smelling of fresh soap and baby oil, she darted quietly past Gayle and reclined sensuously on the couch. "Where's your aunt?" she inquired, crossing her legs.

"Work."

"Aw. She sure is a nice lady. Everybody around here adores her." She looked around and noticed Gayle's music and academic awards on the wall. "Damn, Gayle, you pretty heavy, I see."

"What?"

"I mean, looks like you're pretty talented. I ain't never seen so many awards in one house. You still singin' at church?"

"Yeah. Had a concert last week. It was really good. I'm still trying to get back on track after that one."

"I've always loved your voice. You gotta lot of soul, honey, a lotta soul. Let me know when you sing again. I'd like to come."

"Well, I guess I'll see you Sunday then. I joined one of the community choirs here in town."

"Really?"

"Yeah. We're having our first concert Sunday, and I have to lead a song."

"Aw, yeah. I'm gonna be there."

Sheila had become intensely intrigued with Gayle. She watched the quiet way in which she moved. She saw the sultry sweetness in her eyes. From a distance, Sheila could tell that Gayle had put on a little weight, but she was still sexy. While Gayle sung the last verse of "There'll Never Be," she missed how visibly moved Sheila had become by her voice. She swayed back and forth on the couch and bobbed her head to the music. "They really need a long version of this song. Just in case you wanted to get busy or something." She didn't know she was already listening to it.

"Dinner's ready," Gayle called from the dining room.

Sheila entered the room and gasped. It was simply breathtaking, right down to the fresh oven-baked rolls. "This is so nice, Gayle," she said as she sat down. "You know a perfect

evening is the right kinda music, the right kinda company, the right kinda food, the right kinda breeze, the right kinda…Well, you know," she said, sucking her teeth.

"No, I don't know," Gayle whispered, gazing into Sheila's eyes.

"Never mind," Sheila said as she snapped out of that fantasy just as quickly as she had entered it. "Let's eat."

Dinner was beautiful. They both laughed and talked about everything and, before they knew it, two four-packs of Champales were empty. Sheila certainly drank more than her share. Teddy Pendergrass, Rose Royce, and Marvin Gaye shared in this moment, their voices echoing throughout the room. Sheila gently swayed back and forth as she hummed the words of "I Wanna Get Next to You."

Gayle watched her with an unspoken desire. "You want to sit on the couch?"

"Hmmmm. That would be nice." They moved swiftly to the living room. Sheila said, "It feels so good in here. The air conditioner ain't playin'!"

"Damn, it is kinda chilly in here," Gayle said, hugging her own shoulders. "Let me know if you need me to turn it off."

"Unh-Unh. It's just fine. C'mon over here and sit down. You've been up and down all night." Sheila patted the pillows, gesturing for Gayle to sit next to her.

"You need anything before I take a seat?"

"Any more Champale?"

Gayle brought another four-pack into the living room and watched Sheila down all four.

"Niggaritis has set in. I can barely keep my eyes open."

"You're just drunk, Sheila." Gayle laughed.

"Maybe I am. We'll see later on." Gayle had no idea what that meant. "Excuse me for a minute. I need to go to the bathroom." But before Sheila headed toward the hallway, she stopped at the entrance and asked, "So what's the deal between you and my brother? You dumped his ass after the prom. Left him all heartbroken and shit."

"Yeah, okay. Whatever you say."

Sheila walked up and got right in Gayle's face. Striking a match would have set her ass on fire. "Now, Gayle, you know my brother was poppin' them drawers. C'mon, tell me the truth."

"I don't think that you need to know that right now." Gayle was not ready to tell Sheila that she was actually the one on her mind prom night. "Take yo' drunk ass on to the toilet before you piss on my aunt's floor. It's right next to my room."

"Well, aiight, be that way then. Oh, by the way, when I get back, I got a secret to tell you," Sheila said as she staggered on out the doorway.

Ten minutes had ticked off the clock, and Gayle was hoping that Sheila had not thrown up on the bathroom floor. Now wouldn't that just spoil the whole mood? Damn!

"You okay in there?" Gayle yelled out as she got up to blow out the candles. As she was closing the blinds, she heard the bathroom door squeak open. Finally, she thought. Gayle figured that Sheila might need to leave before she got out of hand. Suddenly, she felt a warm hand on her shoulder, and she quickly turned around. Although night had fallen, the light from the street pole illuminated the nakedness of Sheila's caramel skin.

Sheila pulled Gayle toward her and embraced her with all that was within her soul. When their lips touched, electricity filled with passion entered both of their hearts. Sheila kissed Gayle more sensuously than she had ever kissed anyone. Her heart was beating so fast that it echoed across the room. All of a sudden she snatched away from Gayle.

"We gotta stop," Sheila whispered.

"Huh?" Gayle was sweating profusely and was having difficulty understanding what was happening.

"I said we gotta stop, Gayle. This ain't right."

"What do you mean, this ain't right? You come out here butt naked and start kissing me like I was some niggah, and now you wanna stop?" Gayle plopped down on the couch and just stared at her. "You kissed me, Sheila! Remember that?"

"Yeah, but I didn't expect you to kiss me back." Seemingly disgusted and embarrassed, Sheila headed toward the bathroom as Marvin Gaye started the next verse of "Sexual Healing."

Gayle reached for her arm. "Wait a minute. Sheila," she whispered. "Why did you kiss me?"

She stopped and looked into Gayle's beautiful eyes,

"Because, for some reason, I thought you wanted me to."

"And?"

"I didn't know it was gonna feel like that."

"Like what?"

"Like, you know. It felt good. That shit scared me." Her eyes were beginning to water. "I don't know what I've been feeling. I mean, I know what I been fantasizing about. I think about you morning, noon, and night, Gayle. And I don't understand why. I'm sorry, Gayle. I'm gonna get dressed and head on home."

Gayle walked over to Sheila and held her face in her hands. "You don't have to apologize," she whispered. And then she kissed her again.

Sheila stroked Gayle's breasts, first one and then the other. She kissed every inch of Gayle's face: her eyes, her nose, her cheeks, her forehead, her chin, her lips. She maneuvered her hands underneath Gayle's blouse and unsnapped her bra. After kissing her from her neck to the tips of her nipples, she knelt before Gayle and sucked her nipples like a newborn baby.

By this time, Gayle's juices had run down to her ankles. Sheila pulled off Gayle's shorts, only to discover that her panties were soaking wet. Slowly, she eased them past her ankles and threw them on a chair nearby. As her tongue made its way down Gayle's inner thigh, Sheila tasted her; she wanted her. And there, while on her knees, her tongue entered Gayle, leaving her motionless and speechless. Pulling Gayle to the floor, her kisses saturated her skin. Gayle had never felt such passion.

Gayle chuckled. "You still wanna stop?"

"No, I don't."

They both indulged in ecstasy. Into the early hours of the next morning, they enjoyed one another over and over again. They had shared the right music, the right dinner and, as they both lay across the bed, the right breeze made its way through the window.

Sheila rolled over and hugged Gayle. She smiled and said, "Thanks for sharing my secret."

The strawberry milk, the smoked sausages, and the extra weight meant only one thing. Gayle was pregnant and due in early February. She had no idea who the father was. It could have been

Roosevelt, Bo, or Junior. Since she had kept the events of that Sunday morning to herself, everyone assumed that Roosevelt was the father. During the entire pregnancy, she avoided everyone except Sheila, making her promise to tell no one about the baby, especially not Roosevelt.

▲

Sheila had grown particularly fond of Gayle and was willing to do anything for her little niece or nephew. She bought Gayle everything she and the baby needed. Gayle, however, had other plans. She had already decided to give the baby up for adoption. Because there was just too much heartache surrounding it, she simply could not raise this child, or this bastard, as she often referred to it. Thanks to having five children of her own, Sadie knew that her daughter was pregnant. So, in addition to the care that she received from Sheila, Sadie was also at Gayle's every beck and call. Sadie cooked for her and drove her to every doctor's appointment. On occasion, Gayle hinted that all of the attention was in vain because she didn't intend to keep the baby anyway. Sadie just laughed and moved on. She didn't think that Gayle was that cold. As circumstance would have it, the baby ended up with relatives anyway.

Both Sadie and Sheila were in the delivery room when Gayle gave birth to a little girl. Her pain had been so severe that she'd tuned out the television that was blasting a special report about the investigation surrounding the apparent suicide bombing of an American Embassy in Beirut several hours before. Sheila paid especially close attention to it because Roosevelt conducted a lot of business in the embassy. He'd been stationed there for about two months and couldn't wait until it was time to come home. Sheila left the delivery room and went to find an area with a TV that wasn't so busy.

As she trotted down the hallway to the waiting room, Sheila started having flashbacks about the day she'd gone ahead and told Roosevelt about Gayle being pregnant. Claiming responsibility for the baby without an ounce of proof, Roosevelt was eagerly awaiting the birth of his first child. On this day, though—the birthday of a daughter he truly believed to be his flesh and blood, he had accompanied a friend to the Embassy to pick up a package. A truck full of men dressed in fatigues and black hoods pulled up beside Roosevelt while he waited in the Hummer for his friend. None of the men got out of the covered truck as they shouted what seemed to be foreign expletives about Americans and their government. And like slow motion, they opened their jackets revealing explosives attached to each of their bodies. Roosevelt never had a chance. According to the news report, there were no survivors within a two-block radius.

The nurse wheeled Gayle in from recovery and found a distraught Sheila, with swollen bloodshot eyes, sitting on the bed. She'd just gotten off a disturbing phone call with her father who'd a moment ago been visited by two uniformed Marines on official military business. As she clutched a picture of her and Roosevelt taken the day he had left for the service, Sheila prepped herself to tell Gayle about what had happened. Roosevelt was truly loved by his sister and, in all of his letters to her, he still professed his love for Gayle. Sheila knew there was only one thing she could do.

Shaking Gayle's arm, Sheila whispered, "Gayle, honey, are you awake?" She saw that her eyes were barely open. Her delivery had been a hard one, and those painkillers were keeping her heavily sedated and groggy. "Gayle?"

"A little bit."

"I need to talk to you about the baby."

"What about it? Did she die? I hope she did. I don't want the little bitch."

"What the hell is wrong with you?" Sheila cried.

"I don't want the damn thing. I told you that from the beginning."

"Roosevelt is dead, Gayle."

Gayle did not respond.

"Did you hear me?"

She still didn't answer.

"Gayle, let me have her. Let me raise my brother's child. We won't have to be on welfare and shit like that because me and my family have the cash to raise her."

Sheila knew that Gayle didn't want to bring that baby here as a victim of the welfare system. During their quiet times together, she had always talked about making sure that she and her child did not become statistics. To ensure that never happened, Gayle had prepared to put the baby up for adoption. Out of sight, out of mind.

"Have you lost your mind?" a voice interjected from the doorway. It was Sadie. "That's my grandbaby you're talking about."

"Mrs. Holman, did you hear about Roosevelt?"

"Yeah, I know about that. All the more reason why she should be with me."

Looking over at Gayle, Sheila said, "Well, it is ultimately her decision. The adoption agency called and said that she has two days to change her mind."

"Adoption agency? What the hell have you done to my daughter? You done brought her into this sinful shit that you do, and now you want her baby?"

"You don't know what you're talking about, Mrs. Holman, but now isn't the time to address that."

"How you even know that's his baby? Gayle could've been seein' somebody else."

"I doubt that," Sheila snapped. "Gayle ain't been with nobody but Roosevelt."

Sadie wasn't about to let Sheila get her hands on that baby.

"Stay out of this, Sheila, or..."

Gayle mustered up enough strength to summon the nurse's station, and when the nurse arrived, she asked that both Sheila and Sadie be escorted out of the room so that she could get some rest. And besides that, she had no interest in hearing them discuss her as if she wasn't even there.

The day finally came for Gayle to decide what she was going to do with her still nameless baby. Two days earlier, the adoption agency had received a request, on behalf of the birth mother, to delay the meeting an extra day. Roosevelt's family had decided to go ahead and have a memorial service for him, since his remains would take several days to make it back to Memphis. Everyone needed closure, everyone except Gayle.

She remained in the hospital and considered that chapter of her life almost closed. To soothe her own mind about the issues surrounding her daughter's conception and to bring that heart-wrenching chapter to an end, Gayle signed the baby over to Sheila immediately after the social worker entered the room. It was best for everybody. Doing that, however, Gayle successfully accomplished two things. One was that she would no longer have anything to do with that baby. Within a matter of days, she knew that Sheila would make sure of it. And two, Gayle managed to drive an even wider wedge between her and her mother. Sadie could not understand why her own daughter had betrayed her.

The only comment Gayle made was, "Trust me. Sadie, you don't need that baby or the headache that's gonna come with it."

The child was still her granddaughter, and Sadie couldn't fault an innocent child for its mother's ignorance.

Filled with more anger than one person could ever imagine, Sadie heavily sobbed, "I almost want to say that I'm surprised by all of this, but I'm not. These last couple of years you've been nothing but a disappointment to me—one right after another. You been flauntin' this girl in our faces for months now, without an ounce of respect for us or for her. We ain't stupid, Gayle. We ain't stupid, and I hope you know that. Where was she when you needed money or food in yo' fat ass stomach? I've kept my peace about it because you're my child, but right now, I don't even care about that."

"Momma, let it go. It ain't even worth all that drama you kickin' to me. Besides, all you probably gonna do with that baby is give her away just like you did me."

If she didn't believe that the police would come and lock her up for child abuse, assault, and anything else they could trump up, Sadie would've killed Gayle on the spot. Instead, she sternly said what she thought might be even worse, "You're no longer welcome in my home, Gayle."

With a crisp tongue, as she picked up her overnight bag, Gayle replied, "That's fine because I never was anyway."

14

E
ven though the first morning service didn't start until eight
o'clock, the side parking lot of the church was packed by
seven. A Benz, a Lexus, or a Cadillac was in every other
space. These were the Saints—the Church of God in Christ.
Anybody who was somebody attended the Way of Life Temple. All
totaled, there were over three thousand members and, usually, by
the end of any given Sunday, the attendance was that and nearly
half. Sometimes there were more visitors than actual members.
Sammy, a lot attendant with much attitude, directed parking and
on occasion, if he recognized you, he would get you a space right
up front. If not, you parked on the gravel located a quarter of a mile
from the church's front doors. Everybody wanted to see what went
on in the sanctified church.

"Sister Gayle, how you doin' this mornin'?" He smiled. Sammy,
like many other men in the church, had a thang for her. He stuck
his shiny, bald head just inside her window. "You look mighty
pretty t'day."

"Thanks, Sammy. How you been doing?"

"Well, fairly tolerable, I guess. My arthritis actin' up dis morning."
He waved his arm toward the front. "I saved your spot up there."

"Sammy, you know I got a reserved space." She laughed.

"I know, heh. I just like to see you smile."

"Ol' man, let me get on. I'm running late," she cackled.

He let her pass and went on about his job; giving everybody else hell.

After leaving Mt. Canaan Baptist where she was raised and baptized, Gayle became a member of three other churches. The first was First Progressive Missionary Baptist, which she left because Sheila belonged there. The next was Pleasant Grove, where the first lady of the church ran her out because she found out that Gayle and her husband were doing more than having prayer meetings. And the last was Second Avenue Baptist. Everybody loved Gayle there. That is where she first met Patty and, from that point on, where he went she followed.

Patrick Bennett drove a Rodeo that his mother had gotten for him, and he parked it religiously right next to Gayle on Sunday mornings. Though he and Gayle were the best of friends, he openly despised Chris. It was no secret that the feeling was mutual. The mere mention of the other's name sent each into a mad frenzy. Patty viewed Chris as an educated stuck-up bitch that was out of her league when it came to Gayle. And Chris' opinion of Patty wasn't much better, for she considered him to be a pretentious fag with a fierce obsession for drag queens, $1,000 suits, and blow jobs.

Whenever he came to visit Gayle at their apartment, Chris left the room and, if she were able, she opted to leave the house. Although she proclaimed herself a member of the homosexual community and had a friend in college who was a transvestite, Chris often snubbed gay men, feeling that they were nasty and would eventually contribute to the extinction of the African-American race by sticking their dicks into those dark assholes without faces. Knowing that they were sick, those same men, with no remorse whatsoever, would make a last-ditch effort at normalcy by marrying some unsuspecting woman whose picture-perfect life would forever be turned upside-down. Patty and several of his friends believed that Chris was just using Gayle because whatever Gayle earned, Chris and her children got first. That meant everyone always had to have Gayle's back when they were out, and during those instances when her money wasn't enough, she used theirs to take care of home. Gayle had put herself out on a tremendous limb for that girl. In their opinions, all Chris ever did in return was bitch.

Having met at one of Gayle's Second Avenue Baptist Church concerts, Sunday morning was the only time that Patty and Gayle really got to spend together. During the entire performance, Patrick shouted like a sanctified widow. At every pause, at every "Amen" and after every reprise, he was up and dancing, from the altar in the front of the church to the pews at the back door, testifying for the Lord and giving God the glory. After the concert, he commended Gayle on her performance and asked her out to dinner. He beamed with pride whenever Gayle sang or directed the choir. That was his friend. It was just too bad that she considered herself married to a true bitch.

For the first several months of her relationship with Chris, church was the last thing on Gayle's mind, and so was Patrick. She was almost always tongue deep into Chris' pussy at seven-thirty on Sunday morning. She missed choir rehearsal most of the time and it took the choir president threatening to replace her to make her start attending again. Even then, she sang only by request. To resume her position, she had to be prompt for every choir rehearsal and present at every engagement. This made Chris furious.

"Why don't you come with me?" Gayle would ask. "We can go to dinner afterwards or something."

"Nope. I don't wanna go and sit with a bunch of hypocritical muthafuckas for three damn hours. Half their asses were at the club last night and the other half will probably be at church still wearing their hot pink wristbands showing the 'PAID' stamp when they raise their sleeves to pass the offering tray. And they're usually the main ones up dancing and shit all over the church. You probably right up there with them. No, thank you. I'm staying right here."

"You know that's not true, Chris."

"Bullshit, girl, you've slept with most of them. I really don't wanna sit with your sissified friends to only be informed of who your ex-lovers are."

"You won't even come to hear me sing?"

"I can't even get you to sing here. No, thank you. Besides, I heard your pastor was a faggot. I for damn sure ain't interested in nothing he has to say."

Gayle had heard the same stories about her pastor, but she never bothered to investigate any of them. So what the reverend had busted a few cracks? What person in the pulpit hadn't? The bishop, as most called him, always gave good sermons on homosexuals, and Gayle used that in his defense whenever Chris joked about it. The only comment Chris had was that one speaks best about what one knows.

"Mornin', Gayle! Ain't God good?" Patrick exclaimed as he opened Gayle's car door. His smile was as bright as the sun that morning, but not even the warmth and the beauty of the day could lighten the load that Gayle was carrying in her heart. "Girl, what the hell is wrong with you? Didn't you hear me say, ain't God…"

"I heard you, Patty. I'm not deaf."

"Dayum. What the hell is wrong with you this morning?" he asked. "I hope you ain't takin' this to the pulpit. What did Miss Evilene do today? I don't know why you keep letting her get to you. Ain't nobody's, well, you know, that good. She's just a bitch, B-I-T-C-H!"

"Don't start today, Patty. I ain't even in the mood." Gayle got out of the car and headed toward the building. She exchanged greetings with passersby and walked hurriedly toward the back. Despite the rumors, the members of the church loved her. She was the only person that was ever able to make the choir sing. They rocked in every service and had even been invited to record an album. With her talents, she gave the choir something that it never had before…a soul. They respected her and looked up to her. All of that admiration made the fact that she was gay transparent.

"Did she tear yo' pantyhose again? Flatten yo' tires? Break…" He was on a roll. Chris had a bad habit of doing shit to keep Gayle from going to church and, at first, it worked. Gayle missed choir rehearsal almost every week and then never showed up for church on Sundays. She was totally into Chris. But then Chris' behavior became a pattern. The tantrums worsened, and their relationship was suffering because of it. Sometimes just getting out of the house was a breath of fresh air for Gayle.

She and Chris had become so violent toward each other that it frightened her. The bruises that she left on Chris were often too painful to look at and, sometimes, she would just sit and hold Chris after they'd only minutes ago lit into one another. The scars that Chris left on Gayle's breasts and back were semi-permanent. It would take weeks for them to heal. The worst fight that they had ever had was when Gaylon was two weeks old. Chris had the baby in one arm and was kicking Gayle's ass with the other. She finally put the baby down on a blanket, and they kept at it until Chelsea started screaming and crying. By that time, though, Chris had popped Gayle in the back of the head with a ceramic bowl. Gayle left and stayed gone for almost a week.

Two days before that fight, Chris had come back from the doctor and found a swollen hand print on Chelsea's face. When she asked Gayle about it, she said that the child had fallen. Chris, being red herself, knew what a hand slap in the face looked like. "Gayle, if you hit her, I would like to know." All she wanted was the truth about the whole thing. Maybe she had hit her harder than she'd meant to. But Gayle stuck to her lie. On top of all the other shit, Chris just couldn't take much more.

Many times after that Chris tried to keep Gayle from going to church but, in order to do God's work, Gayle went on anyway and dealt with the consequences later. "You're living with the devil, girl. Get out while you can," Patty teased.

"I think she's going through something, Patty. Don't quite know what it is, but she isn't acting like herself."

"Like hell she ain't!"

Gayle pulled Patty to the side and asked quietly, "Do you remember when you got turned out?"

"Lawd, Lawd, do I?" He laughed, fanning himself with a program. "Miss Thang, lemme tell ya! Had a dick run so far up my ass I was able to taste it. Wooooooo! Bayyyy-by! This ass ain't been the same since!" Patrick noticed the new deacon, Jerome Smalls, walking up. "Pssst, Gayle!" he whispered. "There he is, girl! Look at him! So damn fine!"

"Patty, we're standing at the doors of the church. Watch what you…"

"Gurl, pleeez. My first was a preacher. As a matter of fact, he's a well-known one. Anyway, that deacon's ass is worth burning for! Unh-Unh!"

"Patty!"

"Mornin', Deacon." Patrick grinned.

"Good morning," Deacon Smalls uttered, brushing past Gayle. "You gonna turn it out for us today, Gayle?"

"I'm gonna try. Whatever the Lord wants me to do." She smiled. "Whatever He wants me to do."

"Good!" he shouted and disappeared through the sanctuary doors.

"Honey, honey, honey," Patrick whined as he rubbed his thigh. "It oughta be a sin and a shame."

Gayle thought for a minute. A sin. A shame. She was not equipped to think about it any deeper. "Have you talked to Terry this morning?"

"Sure did. He said he was bringing a friend of his with him. Some girl."

"Aw, well, I need to head to the choir room. I'll see you after service." Gayle disappeared around the corner.

Terry Bishop sang in the Greater Community Workshop Choir with Gayle, and lived around the corner from her and Chris. He was just another shit-startin' queen amongst the rest of them, but he was a pretty one. Wavy, jet-black hair with skin the color of caramelized butter. A baritone in the choir, his voice went from butch to bitch in an instant. He and Gayle had done duets together and hung out at his apartment sometimes to practice, if she couldn't get a note right or if she just wasn't feeling the music. Gayle confided in Terry about her problems at home. Suggesting that perhaps a little outside influence might do the trick, he told her that he had a friend that she and Chris should meet and that maybe a threesome might spice things up a bit.

"No, I couldn't imagine seein' Chris lettin' somebody else do her, especially in front of me," Gayle had told him. "She's too ripe for that and besides, she'd stroke out if she saw another woman touch me. If it were any other woman I'd been with, then I could possibly see it. But, not Chris."

She'd managed to convince Terry that she wanted to work things out at home, but Terry didn't care. On this already dreadful, mind-boggling Sunday, he brought that friend with him, and some shit was about to get started.

"There she go right there, Mimi. See her?" Terry asked.

"Barely." The girl stretched her neck as far as she could until she caught a glimpse of the diva that Terry had been raving about. "I can now. I see her."

Mimi was known for being a shit-starter and seemed to be able to sniff out troubled lesbian households. She'd heard about Chris, through Terry of course, and decided that if Gayle wasn't going to come to her, then she'd go to Gayle.

At the end of service Terry went to the choir room to get Gayle. "Hey, Sugah!" Terry said as he gave her a big, bear hug. "I saw Patty, and he told me that you weren't feeling too well today. From the way you carried on up front, I can't tell you ain't feeling good!"

"It's nothing. Just some problems at home." Gayle saw the girl standing next to him and acknowledged her presence with a nod and a warm smile. "It's all good though."

"Well, I have someone that I'd like for you to meet. Gayle, this is Monica. Monica Upshaw. But I call her Mimi."

Extending her hand, Gayle said, "Hello. Nice to meet you."

"Same here," Mimi said. "You sounded really good up there. I've seen you in concert a couple of times. You're a talented young lady."

The compliments were the easiest way to flirt.

"Look, um, I gotta go," Gayle said, glancing at her watch. "I have another engagement this afternoon."

Pulling a business card from her purse, Monica smiled. "Here, take one of my cards. I do nails in my spare time. Call me if you need a manicure or something."

"Thanks. Nice meeting you." And Gayle was out the door. The last thing on her mind that day was getting her nails done.

"Ain't you going to answer that page?"

Stretched out across the bed looking at television, Gayle's mind was transfixed with confusion, guilt, and a tainted love.

"Gayle!"

"What, girl!" she snapped. "It ain't nobody but Chris, and she don't want shit." The pager went off again. This time she turned it off.

Monica rubbed her back. "You really need to get that. Something might be wrong." She'd been trying to get Gayle over to her house for weeks and then, all of sudden, she'd just shown up one night. Gayle still had no sexual interest in Monica because she was still devoted to Chris. But the constant bickering and fighting was wearing her down. It was wearing both of them down, and in fear of losing what they had, neither of them said a word. Conversation with Monica was a welcomed distraction, but Gayle knew if Chris ever found out, the whole thing would be over.

"I doubt it," Gayle said. "She and her family are probably still waiting on their damn doughnuts."

Gayle kept watching television until after midnight. She kept on thinking about how to fix what was wrong at home. Did she even want to fix what was wrong at home? After years of trying to find someone to replace the love that she didn't get from her mother, someone to replace Sara's benevolent ways, and someone whose presence reminded her of her daughter, she knew that she had found it in Chris. But why then was she so afraid? Gayle knew that Chris loved her. That love finally revealed itself when Chris put her job on the line to help Gayle get out of the shit she had gotten into. Chris had professed the kind of love that nothing could ever take away...even another woman. It was finally unconditional.

SPIRITUALITY IS FOR THOSE WHO HAVE ALREADY BEEN THERE

15

"Are we gonna blow it?" the paramedic asked his partner.

"Probably need to. Her vitals aren't good at all."

The sirens seemed so much quieter when they passed on the streets. John, a ten-year veteran of the fire department, had seen many cases like this one. Some made it. Some didn't.

Department policy required that the fire department accompany the EMTs on all suicide attempts, since time was almost always a concern. You never knew what your situation was going to be. Therefore, being more than prepared was always good. By the time the paramedics got to the door of the apartment, the firemen had already used an ax to break the dead bolt.

Everything was still. There was no power and something in the kitchen had begun to spoil. Boxes were everywhere. It looked as if someone was preparing to move.

"Murphy to dispatch," he radioed in.

"Go ahead, Murphy," the dispatcher responded.

"Are you sure it's number eleven? We're inside, and we don't see anybody."

"Hold on, I still have her on the line." Roberta hated these calls. She always felt so helpless. "Uh, Ma'am, you did say number eleven, right?"

There was no answer.

"Ma'am? You gotta stay with me. Help is there but they're having trouble finding you."

The only thing she could hear was her own voice on all the two-ways in the apartment.

Carefully checking every room along the hallway, the firemen led the way, hoping to find some sign of life.

John, noticing a slightly open door on the other side of the bathroom, was the first to get to the phone dangling from the side of the bed.

"We got her, Roberta. We got her."

Her skin was cold and clammy. Her pupils dilated. Her body was limp and, in her hand, she clenched a picture of herself, two little girls, and another woman.

"Dispatch," he radioed in again."

"Go ahead, John."

"How long did she talk to you?"

"Only for a couple of minutes. I could barely understand anything she said. Did you make it in time?"

"Her blood pressure is sixty over fifty. Pupils are dilated. Low pulse. I'm looking at this bottle of Valium. She took whatever was in here." Feeling through the covers, John recognized the familiar shape of a bottle of vodka. "Roberta, we're outta here stat," he said calmly. "I gotta empty bottle of vodka here, and she's not responding to anything we're doing."

"Age?"

"Mid to late twenties. Got the hospital on the line yet?"

"I'm calling them now. Fire department still there?"

"They're standing here with me. They'll probably be here until someone from the police department arrives. Thanks, Roberta. Don't know what I'd do without you."

So many times Murphy wondered what would bring a person to do this. In this case, the victim knew what she was doing. If she had not made a last cry for help, no one would have found her in time. Because she was now totally unconscious, he knew that the situation was beyond just pumping her stomach.

16

The west wing of Parkside Hospital was reserved for those who required intensive care and needed to be on a twenty-four-hour watch. Most of the patients were there because they posed severe threats to themselves. Inside the television room was a telephone, a few chairs, and a television that was enclosed in a glass case. All meals were taken in this room, and all visitors were received in this room. Just outside the door was the nurse's station where they monitored each patient's comings and goings. Across the hall there were sleeping quarters. Every window had a bar on it, and the only shower stall had no rod and its curtains were made of heavy plastic. The showerhead was three feet above the water controls, allowing no room for a makeshift hanging apparatus.

Ten beds were inside the room. No pillows. No sheets. On the sides of some of the beds were restraining devices. Forget about privacy. Whatever ailments one had, the rest of the room had them too.

Everyone got medicine, or meds, at the same time. Everyone ate at the same time and, unless they were heavily sedated, everyone slept at the same time. Due to the nature of the ward, no one was deprived of sleep.

"Does she have any ID?" the nurse asked. It was just past three p.m., and her twelve-hour shift had just started.

"Yes, here it is," Murphy said.

Looking at her triage report, the nurse commented, "She's had quite a day, huh? Has she been conscious at all?"

"She was for a minute. Long enough to ask what was going on. She barely made it, though."

"You've been with her all this time?"

"Yeah, I asked to be. This one kinda bothered me."

"Why is that?" Selma asked as she pulled back the sheets on the gurney. She couldn't help but notice the outward beauty of this injured soul.

"I don't know. When we picked her up, I was looking around her apartment and noticed that she was an extremely talented woman. Well educated and stuff. She had this clenched in her fist." He handed her the wrinkled picture.

"Has her family been notified?"

"Don't think so. We couldn't find phone numbers or anything. Her utilities were off so it was hard to even see. Do you mind if I hang around for a while?"

"Sure, help yourself, but if you're waiting on her, she'll probably sleep through the night." She looked at the picture and handed it back to him. "Hang on to this for me. I'll get it back when we get her settled."

Murphy just sat there staring at the photo of Gayle, Chelsea, Gaylon, and Chris.

17

The screaming from across the room was too much for anyone to bear, mentally disturbed or not.

"Miss Ruth, you're gonna have to calm down for me, okay?" Selma said calmly.

Her shift had been a quiet one until then. She had spent most of it working with Murphy, trying to contact family members. Miss Ruth was a schizophrenic and was more of a danger to the rest of the unit than she was to herself. Over in the night, she'd steal the other patients' belongings and stash them under her bed. In the next bed was a woman who had insisted that she be killed because she was an alien. She was found lying in the middle of the road waiting to be picked up by her mother ship. The drugs weren't doing anything for her, so they had to tie her ass up. Everybody in that room was under a suicide watch because, within the past forty-eight hours, each one of them had attempted to bring their seemingly miserable lives to an end.

"Excuse me," a faint but groggy voice said. She was trying to get Selma's attention now that the orderlies had strapped Miss Ruth down.

Selma walked over to the bed that had only one sheet on it because over in the night, the rooms were freezing. This newcomer barely had enough life in her to turn over—let alone try to dance with the devil again.

"Oh, I'm glad to see you're finally awake. I had hoped to talk with you before I got off. What do you need?" Selma asked.

"I had a picture..."

Selma reached in her pocket. "Is this what you're looking for?"

"Yes, ma'am. Thank you." It was hard trying to focus, but the images were there. She remembered that they were the last things she had looked at the day before.

"We need to get some information from you, if you're up to it. If not, we can..."

"What do you need?"

"According to the identification we were given, your name is Christian Desmereaux."

Chris smiled. "You got my last name right."

Selma smiled. "French was my minor in college."

"Good choice. It was one of my majors."

"Do you know what happened to you?"

Chris didn't answer. Tears rolled down her face and onto her pillow as she looked at the ID bracelet on her wrist. Nodding her head, she replied, "I think so."

"Okay," Selma said quietly. "You're probably pretty tired right now, so I'm going to let you rest until tomorrow. Is there anyone you want us to call?"

Chris quickly said, "No," and turned her back. Sleep wasted no time coming to her rescue from her dismal world.

The next morning breakfast was brought in, but Chris refused to eat. She did the same thing for lunch and dinner. She was in detox because of the enormous amount of drugs and alcohol found in her bloodstream. By the time she was found by the paramedics, there was no need to pump her stomach because, in an effort to make sure that this was done right, Chris had dissolved all of the medication in the vodka. Doing that, Chris should not have survived.

Dr. Milton Douglass was assigned to Chris, and it was his job to explain the consequences of her actions. To sleep and to cry were the only things she had done while in the unit. No one in her family knew where she was.

"Miss Desmereaux?" he called into the room.

Chris tried lifting her head, but she had become extremely weak since she was not eating. "Yes," she answered.

He walked over to her bed and sat on the edge. "I'm Dr. Douglass, and I'm here to help you. How are you feeling today?"

"Still kinda tired."

"Well, one concern that I have is that you're not eating. I have recommended that you stay in the unit until you eat at least two meals. You need to contact someone to bring you some personal items so that you will be able to move about the unit. Do you need us to call someone?"

"My mother, but I'd like to do it," she said reluctantly.

"That's fine. We have a phone across the hall that you can use." He started flipping through her chart. "You want to tell me what happened?"

"Not really, but I guess that I have no choice."

Chris sat up in the bed long enough to tell him what brought her to the point of self-destruction. To her, it would seem like a lifetime.

"It all started back in March. While I was out of town training for my job, Gayle, my roommate, was arrested for writing bad checks."

"Your roommate?"

"Well, at the time, we were, you know…"

"Lovers."

"Yeah. Anyway, she had gotten them from this friend of hers that always managed to help her find some trouble to get into. I found out that she had lied to me about her involvement, and I was caught between a rock and a hard place, as far as my job was concerned."

"Where were you working?"

"I'm a probation officer, for what it's worth. Most of my time with the company has been spent taking care of my own personal business."

"Are they aware of the fact that you're gay?"

"My supervisor knows. I'll get to why I had to tell her in a minute." Chris sat up and took a long breath. She felt as if she had been run over by a truck. She had no idea what day it was. "Are you sure you need to know this? I mean, it's just a bunch of drama that I'd like to forget."

"Forgetting about it without talking about it will do you more harm than good. Believe it or not, talking about it will help you to forget."

She did wish to get better but doubted if this was going to help. "Well, all right," she said, clearing her throat. "I couldn't understand why she was even writing checks. We had money. She said, however, that she was out buying stuff for me. Everything that she ever got for me was stolen. I appreciated it because she took such risks to get things. I felt like she really loved me to jeopardize herself like that. Last year she was embezzling money from her job."

Dr. Douglass stopped and looked up at Chris. "She was doing what?"

"She had a job working for this office supply company. She was responsible for purchasing from vendors. Once she got the hang of it, she started ordering stuff for other people and even for us. And she was making a killing doing it. For almost five months, she never had less than a thousand dollars in her pocket. She bought everything I needed for my baby, and she kept a roof over our heads."

"But it was all stolen."

"Don't you think I know that?" Chris yelled. "I wasn't raised around that kind of shit! I couldn't even sleep at night for fear that the police or the fucking FBI would turn up at our door. I always felt that someone was watching us. The sacrifices that Gayle made for me and my children made me love her like no other. Eventually,

I started helping her when she needed me, just so I could be a part of her world. In turn, I sacrificed what my family and my education at Howard had taught me."

"So you went to college?"

"Yes, I did. My parents spent close to a hundred thousand dollars on me, and all I ended up with was a fifteen thousand dollar a year job and two children by two different men. You know, it's funny. I saw one of my buddies in Ebony last month. A young leader or something. It fucked with me big time."

"Maybe it's not your time. God tells us when it's time for us to do whatever He has planned for us to do. Just like it was God that saved your life."

Chris cut her eyes at the doctor. "That's another story for another day."

"What is?"

"God."

"Well, we do have counselors."

"No, thank you." She looked at her wrists and at her hands. Maybe if she had slit her wrists she wouldn't have to go through this pain and the humiliation of a botched suicide. "Do you want to hear the rest of this?"

"I sure do."

Gay and lesbian stories always intrigued Milton because they all were the same, just different names and a few times different games. Chris' story, however, seemed to have some depth to it. Her battle was not with this woman. Her battle was with herself.

"Okay." Chris sighed. "During her preliminary hearing, I was afraid that all of that office supply shit was going to come up, but it didn't. She acted as if she wanted to do that whole thing alone. Court and all. I wanted to make sure that she had the best lawyers, the best everything. I helped her to get into school to help her case. Still, after all of that, they wanted her to do some time."

"It was only her first offense. They..."

"No, it wasn't. Standing there in the justice building arguing with her lawyer, I discovered that she had a criminal record. On the way home, she explained to me that she had been arrested before and that there were other things she had done that were not even on there. Shit she had done in another state. I couldn't do anything but cry. It was this woman that I had given up my friends for. It was this woman that I had sacrificed my relationship with my family and my children for. It was this woman that I had stolen for. It was this woman that I had sacrificed my integrity and character for. It was this woman that I had given my life for, but it was also this woman that I had learned to love more than I had ever loved another.

"That same night as we showered together, she told me that she wished that it was just me and her. It was only the second time that I had ever seen her cry. I knew that I needed to give her what she wanted because that was all that she had ever done for me. While we were making love, I told her that I loved her more than she could ever know, and she responded by saying that she loved me more than she could ever understand. She meant that and, although it took me days to comprehend what she meant, it settled in my heart. Our love had touched something in her soul, and I felt like I had conquered the invincible.

"The very next day was a Sunday, and those were the hardest days for me."

"Why?"

"She still loved her friends more than me, and Sundays were the only time they all hung out. She would leave at seven o'clock in the morning and not return until after midnight sometimes. I never understood how she could fuck me and roll over and get up to dress for church. She'd get there and sing and tear the church up. Her friend, Patty, was dating this married minister. He and Patty hooked up on Saturday mornings when the preacher's wife went to the hairdresser. That bothered me. Patty and the rest of the bunch would dance up and down the aisles claiming that they were burning, that they were on fire. They were the first to say 'Amen' and the last ones shouting 'Hallelujah.' The one time I did go with her to church it was as if I wasn't there. I felt like an outcast in their clique. I didn't feel what they felt. I had no emotion. There was no fire inside of me. Watching them showed me how hypocritical they all were. So I quit going.

"This particular Sunday while she was away, I watched the television broadcast of her church." Chris hesitated because she had never told anyone this. "I hated her pastor with a passion. Over the years, I had heard that he was more of a sinner than those he preached to. The pastor before him was in prison for raping teenage boys. I found it incredibly hard to believe that the elders and deacons of the church didn't know what was going on. If you ever asked any of the members about it, mums was the word. And they kept their heads held high.

"Anyway, on this day, I listened to Pastor Booker. His sermon was about the fullness of time. This man knew my soul was in need. He knew that my heart was in pain. Gayle had always told me that I would know when the Lord was talking to me. I wanted to be like Gayle and her friends. I wanted to run up and down the aisles. Then, however, I felt resentment toward Gayle. She had all the religion in the world, but she didn't have an ounce of spirituality. When Gayle came home that night, I tried to talk to her about it, but she went straight to sleep.

"From that night on I was puzzled. I concentrated heavily on my relationship with Gayle, but she started emotionally pushing me away. Later that week she told me that she had to go out of town with her choir. As an attempt to reconcile our relationship, I asked if I could go along but she wouldn't let me. I threw an iron at her and missed. The brawling only stopped when she busted my nose with her fist, but it was the comfort she attempted to give that hurt the most. She left for Arkansas anyway. Two days later her mother told me that Gayle never went out of town. She had spent the weekend with Patty and their crew. I was a nervous wreck because, by this time, the lies had become more frequent, and her love was becoming more distant.

"My family was visiting that Friday night, and Gayle offered to go out and get us some snacks, doughnuts and coffee to be exact. She said that she had to stop at the mall first to get some things for her trip, but she would try to hurry back. That was around eight-thirty. By nine-thirty, no Gayle. The mall had already closed, so I figured that she was on her way back. At a quarter till ten her best friend called and asked me where she was. I told him that she had gone to the mall, but that was well over an hour ago. He called back maybe five or six times. Finally I told him to try her pager. He quit calling after that. Now it was eleven-thirty and still no Gayle.

"My family left, and I waited for another hour before going to bed. At about one-fifteen in the morning, I heard the lock turn, the door was opened and then quietly closed. I heard her hesitate for a second before heading to the bedroom. I had packed all of her bags with all her shit in them. She got in the bed with me and said, 'So I guess you call yourself putting me out.'

"What the fuck does it look like to you?" I asked. "She got up and walked over to the phone and called Patty. I got up and snatched the phone out of the wall and took the receiver also. Gayle was too calm about this, so I told her to take her ass back wherever the fuck she'd come from and never set foot in my house again. She managed to get to the other phone and called Patty again. This time there wasn't an answer, so I assumed he was on his way. Adding to my frustration, she never said a word to me, so I started picking shit up and throwing it outside to help her leave.

"By the time Patty arrived, almost everything she owned was outside on the lawn and on the walkway. A lot of it was damaged from me throwing it. The last thing I threw out of the house was this plant that she'd given me when I'd had my baby the previous fall. The entire scene was right up her alley because she was planning to leave anyway."

The doctor asked, "You have children?"

"Yes, I have two of them. Two little girls."

"How little?"

"About eighteen months apart. One's in Pull-Ups, and the other is in diapers."

Dr. Douglass noted that much of this was postpartum depression. "Go ahead."

"I was so pissed that night. I couldn't even shed a tear. I paged her the next day to come home. I apologized over and over again, even though much of it wasn't my fault. She stayed gone all weekend, so I decided to drive to her concert in Arkansas. Before I left, I stopped by Sadie's. That's her mother. She asked me where I was going, and I told her. Sadie knew that Gayle hadn't been out of town because she'd seen her the day before and, instead of Sadie actually telling me, she called one of Gayle's choir members to confirm that there wasn't a trip that weekend. There wasn't, but there was an engagement that night. I went ahead to the concert as planned.

"It was on that night I was finally able to see and hear Gayle sing. Her melody moved me and inspired me. I looked at her and realized that she had many faults, but she also had many undiscovered and unspoken needs. It was because of these needs that she and I were close to being no more. But something happened that night at the concert. During the altar prayer, Gayle's friend Dexter summoned me to the front of the church. Gayle was on one side of him, and I was on the other. He stood there, holding both of our hands, and prayed with us and prayed for us. They had all been together that weekend, and her friends knew that the end was near. At that time, however, I had to give up. I told God that I was through.

"She finally called that night and told me that she didn't want to be gay anymore. She said that she could never walk in God's kingdom as a lesbian. I had to respect that, and she knew it. She asked to come back home, and I let her. I assumed that she wanted to sleep alone, but she didn't. She came back to our bed, and she held me because she needed to and not because she wanted to.

"The next morning, as we were on our way to work, I confronted her about her trip and her deceitfulness. She turned to me and said that she didn't want to be with someone that had children because kids were a burden. In spite of my driving on the highway in rush-hour traffic, I punched her in the face. She hit me back and busted my lip. Then she opened the door and screamed that she didn't care if she died just as long as she was away from me. I pulled over onto the shoulder to let her out, realizing I had to get a grip because my children were in the back seat. She attempted to cross the highway, but I jumped out and grabbed her." Chris started laughing.

"What's funny?"

It was the first laugh she'd had since she'd been there. "My weave was hanging out the back of my head. She tagged my ass pretty good."

Milton chuckled. "Go ahead, Chris."

"We got back in the car, and I took the girls to daycare, but I couldn't go to work with my busted lip and blood all over me. Instead, we both stayed home and tried to pick up the pieces. The confusing part in all of this was that Gayle still wanted sex from me. She started staying on the phone more and, for the first time, her conversations had become private. She brought the plant that I had thrown out back home, and we tried to save it. I re-potted it and moved it to every spot in the house hoping it would survive. Just like our relationship, it really did try to hang on.

"I wanted to make her happy, so I began writing bad checks to buy her stuff. I'd write the checks and report them all stolen. Because all of this was going through a bank account that I shared with Trey, he pitched a bitch and stopped sending child support money."

"Who's Trey?"

"Chelsea's daddy."

"Gotcha."

"It still wasn't enough. Gayle got to the point where she didn't want to pay any bills. Summer was drawing near, and due to the fact that she felt the rent was too expensive, she emphatically stated that she wanted to move. So I started looking for another apartment. I was uneasy about it because we'd only been in that apartment six months. I loved the scenery with the lakes and the ducks. I often caught Gayle bragging to her friends about this plush place that we had. Right about the same time, Sadie needed Gayle's help. The initial plan was for Gayle to help care for Sara, her aunt. This arrangement was to only be for the summer and would give Gayle's family time to find a full-time nurse. She was supposed to move back in with me after that. But Gayle had other plans. She moved the girls and me into a more affordable apartment about two miles from Sara's house. She got the utilities turned on as well as the phone. Gayle had no intentions of coming back. She never called and was reluctant to come over. She went back to that 'I don't want to be gay' shit and was always on her way to church. She told my mother that I was chasing her and that I was harassing her. She even told her boss that I was stalking her."

"Were you?"

"Probably, but her definition of stalking was for egotistical purposes. My definition of it was to find out the truth. Even though we were practically around the corner from each other, I never saw her. She'd call, and we'd play these stupid games. One night I waited for her at her house. Little did I know that she was waiting for me at my apartment. She couldn't stand for someone else to want me—even though she didn't. And me with my stupid, sprung ass didn't want anyone but her to want me. I stopped eating and, before I knew it, I had lost twenty pounds in less than a month.

"One day I stopped by Sara's and found a blue Honda sitting out front. Gayle came to the door and wouldn't even let me in. She met me at the walk. When I asked about the car, Gayle said that it belonged to a neighbor. I never asked about it again.

"Seeing how vulnerable I could be in the weeks to come, Gayle told me that if I gave her some money to get a car, she would come back home. Not only did I give her money for the car, I wrote another bad check for three-thousand dollars for her to get it. Gayle had no intentions of coming back home or of giving the money back. I never even got a chance to ride in the damn thing.

"Well, last weekend everything began to crumble. The car dealership started calling about the bounced check. If I didn't pay it, they were going to have me arrested. Trey called my mother and wanted to know why I was chasing this woman who didn't want me, why didn't I have a phone, and why was Chelsea not with me. When he found out that Gayle had the phone disconnected because she didn't want me talking to him or anyone else, he lost it. He also wanted to know about the bounced checks that had been running through an account that he and I had set up for Chelsea. Momma started telling half of the shit—in particular the half that she knew nothing about. At no time did she ever ask me what the problem was or why shit had gotten so out of control.

"Sunday night I had a gut feeling about Gayle and her so-called religious rejuvenation. I had been paging her for hours, but she would never return the page. After running out of quarters for the pay phone, I quickly ran up five dollars on my phone card. On the last call, Sadie answered the phone and told me that Gayle had been in and out all day but, the last she'd heard, Gayle was coming back home soon. I figured that I could wait for her and maybe, just maybe, I would find what I had been looking for.

"I'd been there about five minutes when I saw Gayle's car coming up the street." For the first time during the entire hour, Chris started crying. "My heart was beating so fast that I could hardly breathe. Gayle looked me right in the eyes and turned into the driveway. She pulled the car around to the back of the house, and I saw the shadow of a woman enter the side door. Gayle walked over to me and said, 'I told you when you start looking for shit you eventually step in it.' I wanted to kill her. She then said, 'That's my prayer partner. She goes to my church, and we are merely just friends. She is a lesbian, but I'm not fucking her.' That was enough for me because I had said nothing about her fucking anybody. After all, she had told me only days before that she had no desire for sex. The little bit she had gotten, came from me. I believed that but, before I went back to my car, I hit her and spit in her face. The slap was for the bad checks and for the religion she had been looking for. I rushed back home because I'd left the children there alone."

The doctor sat there in disbelief. Here, sitting next to him was a woman, who was obviously very intelligent and very beautiful, that had lost regard for human life because of another woman. He was afraid to hear what happened next.

"I woke up at about four that morning and went to the pay phone, leaving the children behind again. I stopped at a gas station not far from her house and called her to see if her prayer partner was still there. She was so pissed with me that she started telling me what I wasn't ready to hear. 'Yeah, I fucked her. Are you satisfied? Are you gonna stop following me now?' From that moment on, my life would never be the same.

"I calmly sat in my car behind a fence at a nearby store and waited for her to pass by. Once she did, I got behind her and followed her onto the main thoroughfare." Chris sat there staring into space and went on. "At approximately six-forty a.m., I pulled up next to her, rolled down the passenger-side window and yelled, 'The next time you fuck her, think about this!' Without even blinking, I jerked the steering wheel to the right and forced Gayle's car off the road, causing her to lose control, sideswipe a tree, swerve across three lanes of oncoming traffic, and land in the median. Because it was so early in the morning, no one saw me. I made sure of it. I didn't even look back to see if she was hurt. I rushed back home, took my clothes off and got back in the bed and waited.

"About an hour later, there was a knock at my door. I'd been expecting it. I looked through the peephole and saw Gayle and Patty. When I started opening the door, Gayle pushed it and immediately knocked me to the floor. She said, 'Well, in case you were trying to kill me, guess what?'"

"'I really wish you would leave,' I said calmly. 'I've got to go to work.' I hadn't been to work in over a week and was in no condition to go that day either. 'What is he here for? Is he gonna whip my ass or something?'"

"'Bitch, I oughta spit on you!' Patty snapped. 'Didn't she tell you that it was over?' I said, 'No, she ain't got the pussy to tell me that it's really over. She was here just the other day fucking like she ain't never had none.' Patty really laid into me then. 'Well, let me tell you this. She does have another woman. She's been done had one. You're so fucking stupid. Every time you show yo' ass up at church you sit right next to her! And guess what? She ain't got no damn kids!'

"I was crushed. All of my suspicions had been right. I'd been made a fool of once again by someone that I loved. Patty stood there and told me everything while Gayle sat there and listened. He told me that the night that Gayle disappeared—the night she went out for doughnuts—she was with Monica. All of those nights that she was at church…she was with Monica. And the blue Honda…belonged to Monica."

The doctor and Chris had been talking for over an hour, and Chris wanted something to drink. "Can I have some juice or something?"

"Sure. I'll let Selma know what you need." Dr. Douglass headed toward the nurse's station. He stopped just beyond the door and looked back at Chris. "Excuse me, Chris, but do you know a John Murphy?"

"No, I don't," Chris responded quietly. "Why?"

"You have a couple of messages from him. He'd like for you to call him."

"Well, I don't know anyone by..."

Selma interrupted, "He's one of the paramedics that found you. I think that he's just concerned about you. Seems to be a really nice guy," she said, pouring Chris' juice into a plastic cup. "He told me to call him when you were doing better," she continued as she passed Chris the cup.

"Thank you." Chris sipped. "But I'm not ready to talk to anybody yet," she said, cutting her eyes at the doctor.

Dr. Douglass added, "And there is really no rush for you to do it either. We can do this later, if you want."

"Do I have a choice?"

"Well, right now, you do. But sooner than later, you're going to have to talk to me or somebody."

Aggravated by his shitty tone, Chris mumbled, "Let's get it over with."

18

It was especially difficult to talk during the afternoon hours. Everyone in the unit was up and about keeping up shit loads of noise. Chris, at times, seemed frightened by them, but she was afraid to ask the doctor when she could leave. He knew that she was not crazy, and he also knew that her condition was stabilizing but was contingent upon her taking in a meal or two. He brought a chair in with him this time and sat next to her bed.

"You know, Chris. If you eat at least one meal, I'll consider moving you out of here."

"I'll keep that in mind," she said as she watched them give out afternoon medication. Within ten minutes, everyone, except her, would be mellowed out or fast asleep. "You're not putting me on any medication?"

"No," he replied, making notes on Chris' chart. "You don't need that."

"Why not?"

"Honestly, I believe that your state of mind is temporary, so I'm handling your treatment differently. We'll talk more about it later."

"All right. Shall I proceed then, sir?" she joked.

"Why certainly."

"By this time, I didn't know what I was doing. I knew that I needed to get my children away from this, so I took them to my mother's. I tried to tell her what was going on, but she wouldn't listen. She told me that she was sick of Gayle and me, and didn't want to have anything to do with the shit. She said, 'Take your damn kids with you. I didn't help you lie down to get 'em! Take their asses with you!' She loves those kids. I knew that she didn't mean it. Despite what she said, I turned to leave them anyway. She grabbed me by my arm and managed to dig her nails into my skin. The more I pulled the more my skin tore. Once she let go, she pushed me to the floor and started punching me in my back. When I tried to get up, she grabbed me around my neck and pushed my face to the floor. Flashbacks of me and Gayle hit me like lightning."

"Must have been painful for you. Going through that with your mother."

"This whole thing has been frustrating for both of us. I'd gotten to the point where I felt like I deserved to be hit. I took the beating and, when I finally got up, I told her that she was just like Gayle. She couldn't wait to kick my ass in front of my children. She started crying and walked away from me. I ran out the door, stormed to the car, and got all of their shit out and threw it on the lawn. They didn't have any clean clothes, and Gaylon didn't have any milk. At that point, I didn't even care. I drove away in search of the woman who'd left me because I had children."

"Are they still with your mother?"

"I guess so."

"Good." Dr. Douglass had children of his own and could never see himself doing this to them but then again, he wasn't Black, he wasn't a woman, and he wasn't gay. Some types of betrayal are hard to forgive.

"I went to see my daddy, the second man that I'd learned to disrespect."

"Who was the first?"

"The man that used to be married to my great-grandmother. He died some years ago."

"What happened to make you disrespect him?"

The tears started again, but this time Chris got sick to her stomach. "Can you hand me that garbage can over there?" He gave it to her just in time. The juice came up, and she dry-heaved for almost five minutes. "Your body's still in shock. Want some water?"

"No, this isn't any damn shock! I hate that muthafucka! Just the thought of him makes me sick! For close to seven years, he molested me. He touched my breasts and once, while I was sick, I really believe that he raped me. Although it started when I was nine, I didn't tell anyone until I was well into my teens. I kept quiet because, at that time, child sexual abuse wasn't really a big deal. He almost died once, and I didn't want him to die without facing what he had done. So I told my daddy and begged him not to tell my mother because she was crazy about that old fucka. He told her anyway, and they both believed that his illness was punishment enough for him. Neither one of them said anything to him.

"Unfortunately, he didn't die, and, not even a week after his ass was out of the hospital, he started fucking with me again. This time my mother told my great-grandmother, who, as I already knew she would, called me a liar. From that point on, I vowed to never tell my parents anything because they didn't know how to handle it right. I wanted his ass in jail, but no one ever did anything to him. When confronted, he said that I was lying. By this time I was old enough to stay home alone whenever my great-grandmother and my mother went out. It didn't matter anyway.

"He died when I was a senior in high school, and I was responsible for breaking the news to the other children in the family. The blow came, though, when my parents, well—actually my daddy— made me go to the funeral...out of respect for the family. Hell, I didn't even go to my great-grandmother's funeral when she died a year later. That's what helped my daddy get his second place rating. Since then his constant flock of women, inclusive of his new wife, has moved him into first place on many occasions. He's the reason I started loving women. I refused to be deceived by any man."

"Did you ever get counseling for the abuse?"

"Nope."

"I see."

"So, anyway, I went to see my daddy. When I got to his shop, he wasn't there, so I went to his office. I looked in his desk drawer and found what I was looking for and left. I wanted her dead, Dr. Douglass, but I still loved her. I'd still do anything for her. I made it to the bank and cashed one of my daddy's checks for a thousand dollars."

"Did you forge his signature?"

"No, it's too hard. He damn near draws his name as it is. It was already signed. Before leaving the bank, I called Gayle and told her that I had some money to get her car fixed. She said that she didn't care and preferred not to be anywhere near me."

"Can you blame her, Chris? You could've killed her."

"She'll be all right. Trust me. The car didn't sustain a lot of damage. It's raggedy as hell, but it still runs."

"How do you know?"

"I'm getting to that. Later that night she paged me and left a text message saying to meet her down by the river. I jumped out of bed, got dressed, and rushed down there. When I saw her, I was relieved to see that she still had some love for me. She hadn't turned me in to the police, and she was still willing to see me. We sat in her car, and she began telling me about Monica. That was the most painful thing for me to hear, but I needed confirmation of when, where and how Monica came into existence. She'd met her the same Sunday that I'd watched that broadcast on television. It's funny. Shit hadn't been right since then. Anyway, the more I listened the more disgusted I became. I found so many faults within myself that I failed to realize Gayle's true self. I wondered how I could have wanted her dead when she seemed to love me enough to tell me the truth and to want better for me by sending me and my love away. She flatly told me that she was afraid of my kind of love and, when she saw on that night in March that I loved her as unconditionally as I did, she knew that it was time for her to walk away. I gave her the money and got out of the car. How do you love someone who punishes you for loving them?"

Chris was crying so hard by this time that Dr. Douglass wanted to stop.

"We can stop for today, Chris. You need to get some rest. You've been through a lot."

"No, I don't want to stop. I'm almost done."

"Okay," he said pleasantly. "Go ahead."

19

The afternoon snacks were brought to the unit and, after catching a glimpse of Miss Ruth drooling over the fruit cups, Chris graciously passed hers along to her. "When can I go home? I can't stand being in this room, " she whined to the doctor.

"As soon as you begin to cooperate a little bit more, we can talk about that. Finish what you were telling me."

"The next morning it hit me that I'd tried to kill someone. I actually had it in me to want to kill someone. It felt like I was being driven by something more powerful than man himself. I just lay there in bed and asked whoever was listening to protect me and to guide me because I was no longer thinking as myself. After that I called the phone company from my house."

"I thought the phone was off?"

"They got this new thing now where you can only call the phone company or 9-1-1 when the phone is off."

"Oh, I didn't know that."

"I called the phone company to see how much I had to pay to get my own service. They wouldn't let me access the account because Gayle had put a code on it to prevent me from knowing anything about the bill. So I sat in my apartment and looked at the walls until it got dark. I was helpless. I had no money, no family, no friends. I went outside to check on my plant that I had been nursing. With all the drama and shit, I failed to realize that the damn thing was dead.

"Wednesday, I decided that I wanted my babies with me. If all else failed, I'd still have them. I went to a pay phone and called my mother to tell her that I was on my way. She told me that I had to have the police with me if I wanted them back. No problem, I thought. I got to her house with a sheriff's deputy and two other officers by my side, and she let them in but not me. They were in there for quite a while, and some other squad cars pulled up. I knew she'd been in there telling half shit again and, by the time it was all over, they made me leave the children. I visited with them for two minutes or less and was asked to leave. They escorted me back to my car, and I went to call the only person I wanted to be near. Gayle.

"She was at home but was quick to tell me that she was on her way out. I told her what had happened and, for a split second, she seemed to care. She offered to come over later on. It was close to midnight when she got there. When I opened the door, I could smell the liquor on her, but I didn't even care. She stopped just inside the doorway and looked into my eyes. She tried to kiss me, but I turned away. I told her that I could not kiss her knowing that she had kissed another, and I felt the same way about fucking her. She wanted to anyway. Inside, this whole scenario felt like good-bye. She told me that Monica was never affectionate with her and that she never seemed to love her as I did. I explained to her that Monica was a choice that she'd made, and she had to deal with it. As she took off my robe, she reminded me of something I'd said to her one night when we were fighting. I never knew that she even paid me any attention then. On this particular occasion, I'd told her that seafood to her would always be Captain D's or Red Lobster. She lacked culture and would never know the delicacies of fine dining because she was too ghetto and too ignorant to try something new."

"Damn, that was kinda low, wasn't it?"

"Uh-huh, but it was true. We've never been compatible. Never will be. That's hard to deal with when you really love someone. Anyhow, I let her get on top of me, and I let her make love to me. Tears streamed from the corners of my eyes while I just lay there. She asked me what was wrong, and I reminded her of her deception. She climbed off and put her clothes on. As she was leaving, she told me that she would always love me. She apologized for hurting me and for destroying my life. It was the only time that we'd cried together, and it felt so real to me. We embraced each other and sobbed until we felt in our hearts that we had to let go. I asked her if I could see her to the car, but she insisted that I didn't need to. Then she walked out. I turned the light on to lock the door and found her keys on the floor. The closer I looked at them the more I realized that they weren't her keys. I opened the door and ran to the alley where she usually parked. And there she sat in the blue Honda with Monica on the passenger's side.

"In the back seat were Patty and Dexter. Patty said, 'Hey, Miss Prissy. Gayle just gave Monica a slammin' ass birthday party at the Radisson. Wish you could have been there.' His hatred for me was most evident then because he knew that I had just given Gayle a thousand dollars. I went upstairs and opened my kitchen cabinet and found a bottle of vodka. Then I went to the bathroom and pulled out a nearly full bottle of Valium that I'd gotten some time ago from my doctor. I dropped the pills in a glass and poured vodka over them. As I walked toward the bedroom, I remembered one day when I was at my mom's house. Chelsea was about ten months old at the time. Momma always kept pictures of me around the house, and it was easy for anybody to see that throughout the years I always looked the same. Anyway, Chelsea walked over to a picture of me that was taken when I was in junior high school. Momma asked, 'Chelsea, who is that in that picture?' Chelsea took her little stubby finger and pointed at me. 'Mommy!' she shrieked. I never realized that my child knew who I was. I always believed that deep down inside she resented me for putting Gayle before her. I felt like she knew her mommy was hurting. Shit, there were even times when I knew that my baby was comforting me. I was just too cold and too emotionally torn to know it. Then, almost within the same tick of a clock's second hand, I imagined my children's last memory of their mother being my body in a casket. They'd have to live with that the rest of their lives. My babies wouldn't be able to understand that they would never see me again. Only in pictures would they be able to remember me, and being in a casket—dead from both an abused heart and soul—was not how I wanted my children to remember me. Soon after that, this pain shot through me. It was worse than labor. I had a picture of us sitting next to my bed, and I held it as I drank my concoction. At exactly midnight my utilities were turned off. Next thing I remember, I was here."

"I see," Dr. Douglass responded. Milton, a tall, well-groomed man with a Harvard degree, was attracted to something within Chris. But she already had a lot on her plate. The last thing she needed was something else to digest. Besides, he had a duty and it was time for him to perform it. Maybe in a year or two, he thought. "Well, you've surely given me an earful. You can be sure of that. Let me tell you what I see, and this is off the record. The main issue that you have yet to deal with is the sexual abuse you sustained as a child. You've never dealt with it and, whether you realize it or not, it has affected almost every move you've made. It's going to take several sessions to get you to that point. Next, you've had two children in less than two years. You're probably still going through postpartum depression. Some time away from the children may actually do you some good. Your dad, your mom, and a number of other things will have to be dealt with in time. Now this woman that you've been telling me about, you need to leave her alone. She should probably be in here in the bed next to you. She's an example of a person who has self-destructed and is too stupid to notice it. She's walking around and leaving those destroyed pieces of herself with people and not one of those pieces is any good to anyone." Dr. Douglass knew that he'd just violated every ethic that he'd been taught but, under the circumstances, he didn't care. "Now for the record," he said, clearing his throat. "Our standard treatment for depression can last anywhere from three days to several months to several years. It just depends on you."

There were many initial approaches to treatment that would've worked for Chris, but she chose two of them that only made matters worse. The call to her mother got her the response she'd anticipated. Ora was pissed for having to change her schedule to take care of her grandchildren while their mother sat in the nut house. Never knowing how to communicate with Chris, Ora just slammed the phone down and painfully went about her business. Like a warrior armed for a mind game with the enemy, Chris was now ready to talk to Gayle—the second mistake. Dr. Douglass had cautioned her about calling Gayle because it would hold up any progress.

"I need to call her," Chris has insisted.

He couldn't stop her, and he knew she would be in for more heartache. She, on the contrary, felt that Gayle would be pacing the floor by now wondering where she was. The phone rang three times before someone answered.

"Hello."

"What are you doing?" Chris asked.

"Nothing. Where are you?" Gayle asked coldly.

"In the hospital. I'm out at Parkside."

"The crazy house?"

"It's not a …"

"Yes, it is. What the hell are you doing out there? I just know that you didn't try to kill yourself." There was silence on the other end of the phone. "Chris, you hear me?"

"Well, I did," Chris said softly.

"You 'bout a stupid bitch. Trying to kill yourself over this shit. It's all just a game, Chris."

"I could care less who you fuck, Gayle. It isn't about that. The problem I have with you is that you lie too much. You told me that you didn't want to be gay anymore because you wanted to get your life right with God. Instead, you went out chasing some other pussy. I probably could have taken you telling me that as opposed to blaming it on religion."

"Girl, whatever," Gayle snapped. "You take shit too seriously. That's one of the reasons I didn't even want to be with you. Always trying to figure out something. You're too damn smart for your own good. Got all the book sense in the world and not a lick of street sense. Damn, you can't even kill yourself right."

It was as if the devil had revealed himself, for those words were the meanest that anyone had ever spoken to Chris. The only reply she could give was, "I'm glad I didn't kill myself right because I would have never gotten to see just how much of a true bitch you are. Thanks for your kind words." And then Chris gently put down the receiver.

She never knew that trying to love a woman would be so difficult. Chris didn't know how to love her mother because her love for Ora was always measured in gifts and shopping sprees. And loving Gayle had been absolute shit. She couldn't remember a time when they'd ever been happy for more than a day or two at a time. Her stint at Parkside had some underlying purpose, and it was now up to Chris to reveal its meaning.

▲

Gaylon and Chelsea each reflected a part of their mother's personality. Chelsea was cool with being with Grandmomma Ora because she got her way and got everything she wanted, raising plenty of hell when she didn't. Gaylon needed her mother but wasn't able to reach her because that bond wasn't there. Chris was like that. She and Ora never bonded with each other, making Chris look elsewhere for the compassion not readily given by her mother. Could that be why she desired and needed another woman's love?

Promptly returning phone calls was something that Darcy just didn't do. Weeks would pass before she even checked her voice mail. When she finally checked it, after returning from yet another trip to Philly, she noticed that there were at least two calls from Chris almost every day. The date stamps let her know that she'd called constantly for over a week. The tone in Chris' voice weakened with each call, and it was the last one that made Darcy pick up the phone. "Darcy, I'm just so tired of all this bullshit. Trey doesn't want and can't stand me. I fucked up his life along with my own. If he'd just wanted me like...like..." In between sniffling and weeping, Chris continued, "I know what I need to do to make it all go away." But when she called Chris' house, she got a recording stating that the phone had been disconnected. She frantically flipped through her organizer knowing that a mother always knew how to find her child.

"Hello."

Whew, her number was still the same. "Ms. Desmereaux?"

Ora was still miserably upset about Chris' call. "Yes?"

"How are you? This is Darcy. Chris' friend from Howard?"

Finally someone with some sense. "Oh, hi, baby. I'm okay. How you doing? It's been such a long time since I've heard your voice."

"I'm doing well. I was calling because..."

"I know. You're looking for Chris."

"Well, yes, I am. She left some messages for me, and they've got me a little worried. Now her phone is disconnected."

Retreating to the bathroom in the back of the house for some privacy, Ora told Darcy as much as she knew and didn't consider whether or not it was the truth. Her baby was hurting and was now emotionally withdrawn from the entire family. She had to grasp the reality of the fact that she had played a major role in all of it. "So that's it. She's gotten herself caught up with these people who only care about playing with her mind. Ain't none of them got shit going for them. By the way, have you by any chance talked to Trey?"

"No, ma'am. I was about to ask you the same thing."

"He hasn't called here, and this baby of his is starting to look just like him. You know, Chris will probably never be right because of that breakup."

"You're probably right, Ms. Desmereaux. I've known Trey for a long time and would have never thought that he'd be acting like this. It may seem like he's hurting Chris on purpose, but I really don't think he is. He's just not that kind of guy."

"Well, what would you call how he's behaving?"

"Just being young and stupid, that's all. He doesn't know any better."

"Well, he sure is missing out on the best times of this baby's life."

Darcy abruptly cut Ora off. The conversation was going in a direction that she didn't want to touch... yet. "Okay, well, I'm glad I found your number, and I thank you for telling me everything. I'll be in touch." Darcy's own world was hectic enough with her trying to relocate and everything, and the last thing she needed was another distraction.

20

Chris needed to confide in someone. Darcy hadn't returned any of her phone calls, so she'd given up hope of hearing from her any time soon. After hours of insomnia and tears, she could not figure out why God was allowing this to happen to her. She had seen that Gayle was nowhere near the spiritual person that Chris had believed she was. The next person she thought of was Patrick.

As soon as the phones were turned back on that morning, Chris called over to The Way of Life Temple and asked for a listing of the new deacons. Patty, who had been desperately trying to get into bed with that new deacon with the tight ass, figured that the smartest thing to do would be to express an interest in becoming a deacon. After days of coming in and out the church for something other than good music and holy dancing, Patty realized that he actually liked it. The funny thing was that Patrick could now quote and extrapolate a scripture quicker than most preachers. He knew his shit.

"Good morning, Way of Life," a woman's voice answered.

"Uh, yes," Chris said, clearing her throat, "I'm trying to reach Patrick Bennett."

"Who?"

"Patrick…"

"Oh, oh, I'm sorry, honey. You're talking about Deacon Bennett. He's not available, but Elder Murphy is here."

"Who's that?"

"Every new deacon is assigned to an elder of the church for guidance and whatnot. It's my understanding that Mr. Bennett's mother died a few days ago."

"Really?"

"It was kinda sudden. Elder Murphy has been covering things for him until he comes back."

Chris had to think. She reverted back to her original thoughts. She still needed to talk to someone. "I guess that I could talk with him."

"Well, you can come here, or do you want him to come to you?"

"I think that it would be best if he came to me." Chris gave the secretary the information she needed and was told to expect him later on in the afternoon.

Once again, Chris rejected dinner. At this point she had too much on her mind to eat.

"Chris," Selma called. "You have a visitor."

"All right."

"Are you sure you want to see him?" Selma remembered Elder John Murphy from when he had brought Chris into the wing. "It's the man I told you about."

Chris then realized why the paramedic had wanted her to call. He was a messenger of God. "Okay, I'll be right there." She wrapped a sheet around her shoulders and walked to the lounge. "Hi, I'm Christian Desmereaux." Her rigid spirit was still thawing, but she forced a smile anyway.

Although her eyes had dark circles around them and her lips were dry and cracked, Elder Murphy was stricken by Chris' strong presence. She moved slowly but gracefully and still displayed the most beautiful smile that he'd ever seen. "Hi, I'm Elder John Murphy. It's nice to finally meet you. I didn't think that you were going to make it."

"Sometimes I wish I hadn't," she said softly, biting through the broken skin on her lips.

"You shouldn't say that."

"I think that the pain and embarrassment from surviving this thing is worse than what drove me to it in the first place."

"Why do you say that?"

"I talked to her the other day, and she told me that I couldn't even kill myself right," Chris said as she glared at the floor.

"Who said that to you?"

"She did." Chris went on to tell him who "she" was to her and everything about her ordeal. Their conversation lasted for hours, and, just before Selma led him out of the lounge at the end of visiting hours, Chris asked, "Have you ever noticed that whenever people who are near death talk about a bright light, they always speak about being close to heaven?"

"Yeah, and?"

"Well, think about this. How many people have you heard say that they were almost in hell and got to come back?"

▲

The third-shift nurses were not the friendliest women. They were jovial amongst themselves, but to the patients, they were like wardens. Each was talked to like a slave without papers, and each was made to remember that it was his or her own fault that the unit was now home. Zena was the only one that would bend the rules every now and again by allowing late night snacks and sometimes a visitor—depending on who that visitor claimed to be. While she was in the reception area gathering magazines for her coworkers to read, she heard tapping on the front door of the lounge. She cautiously proceeded to the door and found a woman who was apparently ignoring the fact that the facility was closed.

Nestled in the corner that surrounded her bed, Chris had almost rocked herself to sleep when she suddenly felt someone standing over her. She thought that Miss Ruth was there again, looking to take away some of her personal belongings and chant over her. Chris didn't budge until there was a tap on her shoulder and, as scary as Miss Ruth appeared, she lacked the courage to lay a finger on anyone.

"Chris, honey, are you asleep?"

Chris rolled over and looked into Zena's violet eyes—well, her violet contacts. Zena was a stout, attractive woman whose mocha chocolate complexion had no business being matched with contacts that color. "Almost. Why?"

"There's a lady here to see you. It's after normal visiting hours, but she said she's your sister. I've got a real soft spot for family."

Iysha? Something had to be up because Chris knew that there was no way in hell that Iysha was ever going to come out there. For an instant, it crossed her mind that it might be Gayle. "Okay, thank you." Her hair was still wet from an earlier shower, so she wrapped herself in her blanket that felt like burlap brushing against her skin, pulling the blanket to just about the back of her head. The temperature in the unit seemed to always be below freezing. Zena escorted her to the lounge, but Chris didn't see Iysha. Instead, pacing the floor with folded arms, was an obliviously exhausted Darcy.

"I knew you should've stayed in D.C.," Darcy said as she embraced Chris. "This would've never happened if you had." Darcy had dropped everything and taken a flight out the morning after she'd spoken with Ora. The two friends stood there holding each other. "I got on the first thing leaving out of D.C. after I talked with your mom," she said, pulling a tissue from her purse.

"Did she ask you to come?"

"She didn't have to."

Chris slowly moved toward the sofa to take a seat. Her knees were still wobbly, and the room never seemed to be still. "I don't even know where to begin."

Pulling a chair up to look Chris straight in the eyes, Darcy suggested, "Let's start with getting you out of here. You don't need to be in this place. You've made me realize how triflin' it is of me to not check my messages."

Chris couldn't muster up the will to smile. She placed her head on Darcy's lap and sobbed. "I've made such a mess of things, Darcy."

"No, you haven't. Some very mean people and shitty circumstances forced you here. You're just a victim of some horrible circumstances." Darcy had already concluded that Chris was driven to this because she felt that she had no way out, and that every human being responsible for her being in the hospital was now sitting somewhere trying to judge her. "Have you ever mentioned this girl to me?"

"No. I started to the night I told you about that white woman, but I figured that one was all that you could handle."

"We're friends, Chris. You should've never thought that."

"Besides, at that time, I had no idea that things would turn out like this."

"You told anyone else from school?"

"No. I'm too ashamed, and I really haven't been in the mood for a bunch of lectures. You didn't tell Trey, did you?"

"Girl, no. His ass is part of the problem, too. You've had so much on your plate these last two years, and instead of trying to be there for you, he just ran further and further away. Oooo-wee! I could just step all up in his ass right now! He hasn't called or anything?"

"No." Chris pulled herself together and took a moment to be absorbed in the presence of a welcomed friend. "Thank you for coming down here. I know..."

Darcy was fuming as she watched one of her closest and dearest friends almost on the verge of blowing her brains out, if she'd had the nerve. Where did everything go wrong? "We've got to get you better so that you can get out of this place, and then we've got to get you away from this city and these people."

"Can I ask you a question?"

"Yeah, anything. Chris, please ask me anything."

"How do you feel about God and church?"

"Well, anything but that."

"Why not that?"

"Because that's the one thing that should always be personal. Just like it ain't nobody's business what you do in your bedroom. Religion is between you and God." Darcy hesitated for a second and took Chris' hands into hers. "I will tell you this. He's all around you in here. I can feel it. Right now, your soul is wide open. It's vulnerable, and that's how it needs to be. God started helping you the first time you called me. When my stupid ass didn't call you back, He stepped in again by helping you call 9-1-1. Then He stepped in again when He sent that nurse up front to get those magazines; otherwise I'd still be up there knocking on that damn door. Do a couple of things for me, Chris."

"What?"

"Read the 23rd Psalms whenever you think about that girl. When I felt like things weren't going right, I picked up the Bible and just started reading. I mean, I read scriptures that reflect life— almost everything we do or say has something to do with the Bible. Psalms 23 has kept me from kickin' a-many-a brotha's ass when I just couldn't take the bull anymore. It's kept me from walking off a-many-a jobs, too. Then, after you do that, there's one more thing."

"What?"

"Even though you two have had your share of problems, tell your mom that you love her because I know that she loves you."

"Okay, I will."

"Anything else?"

"I love you, Darcy."

"I love you, too, Chris, but you know I ain't with that kinky shit, right?" She laughed.

"Aw, now, ain't nothin' wrong with havin' a little freak in ya!" The laugh was weak, but still, it was there.

Darcy panicked.

"Girl, please. You ain't my type no way," Chris teased. "You ain't got enough booty for me."

Darcy jumped up and fanned her butt in Chris' face. Sliding the palms of her hands down her slender torso, she smiled. "Is that what it is? Is that why I can't get no man?"

Chris rose from her seat and hugged Darcy. Kissing her on the cheek, she whispered in her ear, "I needed this so much. Thank you again for coming."

There was a lot that Chris hadn't told Darcy, but now it didn't matter. Darcy rushed back to the airport to return the rental car and catch the next flight out for Washington at six a.m. She'd sleep on the plane. She had to be back in Philly by that evening to sign the lease on her new apartment.

21

Prior to this week, Gayle had refused to ever set foot in First Progressive Missionary Baptist Church. She'd risk seeing Sheila and other memories that she had thrown away. But this week she was asked to sing at the funeral of a teenage girl that had been gunned down on her way home from school. Since some had said it was possibly gang-related, there had not been much media coverage about it. The victim had been a thirteen-year-old honor student who was in the wrong place at the wrong time. Gayle, caught up in singing for egotistical purposes, didn't like singing at funerals because there was so much emotion involved. And this one, at the moment, didn't appear any different.

She'd arrived just before the casket was brought in and, for some reason, there was an energy that she couldn't fathom. She felt like a lost part of her was someplace close by. As the family filed in, Gayle recognized the gentleman that escorted the other two ladies in the front. He had grown a beard, which was graying like the rest of his hair, but his facial features were still the same. The striking resemblance between him and his son was still there and, had his son lived, they could have passed for twins. When the two women got to their seats, they removed their veils. It was Sheila and her mother. Soon after, the casket was opened, and Gayle found the part of her that had summoned her soul to the altar.

Meisha Alese Harper had grown up believing that Sheila was her natural mother. They had some of the same physical features and some of the same mannerisms. They loved the same things and always shared their deepest secrets. Still, however, there was one secret that Sheila had never shared and that was the true identity of Meisha's mother.

Not many knew that Gayle was Meisha's mother. Those who did know never said a word because Gayle had such a horrible reputation. Over the years, she had dogged many people for no reason. Family. Friends. Lovers. She ran from love like Superman from kryptonite. Whatever she touched she destroyed, and never felt any remorse for having done so. She gave her child away because, to her, it represented uncleanliness. Conceived from rape, she never thought it could symbolize any kind of love that she would ever know or even want to know. And until today, she had never laid eyes on her daughter to see that she looked just like Roosevelt.

To Gayle the lifestyle was filthy, but it gave her a false sense of security that was validated by her attendance and participation in church. She knew where it was written that homosexuality was an abomination against God. She knew where it was written that we fight against principalities. She knew more than she wanted others to know that she did. The church songs that she sang so flawlessly never reflected what was in her heart. Only what the rest of the world wanted to hear. She didn't want to be considered a spiritual person, only somebody who had good religion.

But as she looked at the tranquil composure of her daughter, she realized that her religion was of no use to her. She needed the spirituality that she had alienated from her life. Now was the time for the answer to Chris' question, but the words would not come. Only tears. Fourteen years of suppressed tears. The one person who would understand her held, at this moment, more contempt for her than any other human being had. Well, maybe with the exception of one. And that was Meisha.

Meisha had found out, by accident, that Gayle was her mother. Her sociology teacher had given her class an assignment that involved creating a family tree and tracing bloodlines. Sheila had promised her that she would help her once she got in from work, but, on this particular day, she was running late. Meisha wanted to get started so that she would be able to watch television before she went to bed. She headed toward the attic where Sheila kept all of her personal records and even some of her private things. While going through a box, which contained Sheila's yearbooks, she found, stuck between the senior superlatives, a letter addressed to Sheila and inside of it was a folded note. The letter read:

Dear Sheila,

I hope that you are doing well. It is hard to believe that you are graduating this year! I wish that I could be there to see you on your prom night and to see you march down the aisle on graduation day. I still remember how you just stared at Gayle and me on our prom night. I hate to admit it, but I think that she had someone else other than me on her mind that night. I mean, we had a good time and all, but she just seemed to be somewhere else. Anyway, I made love to her that night like a true playa would have. Thanks for telling me that she's pregnant. I know that she wouldn't have ever told me. You know how sometimes you just get a feeling that something good's about to happen to you? That's what I'm feeling. I'm pretty sure that the baby is mine. I gots some pretty potent shit down there! She's treating me like I'm the salt of the earth, but regardless of that, I still love her. Enclosed in this letter is the name of a doctor that is storing a sample of my blood. After the baby is born, see if Gayle would agree to take it by there to have a blood test done. She might need to give blood, too. The doctor is real cool and knows what's up. I just gotta know, Sheila.

I used to love to hear Gayle sing because she did it with so much feeling. She made you feel every note and every word. If she had married me, I would have wanted her to sing at our wedding. But I guess that will never be.

It's lonely over here, but I am comforted by a spirit that is somehow connected to me. It keeps me going in this wretched place. If that baby is mine, tell her I love her and that I will see her soon. If she's not, tell her anyway.

Love always,

Ro-Ro

P. S. I know it's a girl. That's what God had always promised me.

The guy in almost every picture was Roosevelt Harper, and in one of them was Gayle Evans. Meisha unfolded the enclosed note, along with her birth certificate attached, that coldly read:

Here is a corrected copy of her birth certificate. It's got Roosevelt's name on it along with mine. Also here is my blood donor card with my blood type on it; just in case you ever need it.

Love,

Gayle

When Sheila got home that night, her daughter confronted her about the papers in the attic, inquiring if she was ever going to tell her.

"I was going to tell you, when the time was right."

"Well, the time is right now, Mommy. I'm old enough to understand this."

Sheila sat down with Meisha and told her everything. She explained that she and Gayle had been lovers once and that she and Gayle hadn't spoken since she was a little over a month old. Just after that the doctor was contacted, and a DNA test was done, proving that Roosevelt was indeed her father. It was an amicable parting of ways between Gayle and her and, given the circumstances, it was for the best. Also Sheila explained that she had seen her real mother on many occasions—most of those times being at church when the Greater Community Workshop Choir sang. Her mother was the woman that brought the church down and brought the sinners to their feet and then to the altar. Her mother was the one that everyone talked about…good and bad. But she didn't care about that. All she knew was that she had another mother and, as she reached over to hug Sheila, she thanked the Lord for giving her two of them. Walking toward her room, she turned and asked, "If that's the case, do you think that she ever loved me?"

Sheila cleared her throat. "I really don't know, baby. That's something only she could tell you."

"Well, promise me this. If anything ever happens to me and I must go before you, I want her to sing at my funeral. I'll have peace knowing that she did."

When Sheila had Pastor Jordan call Gayle, she insisted that she not be told whose funeral she was attending. Upon her acceptance, Sheila knew Gayle would have sung merely because she had to perform for God. It never would have been to lay a soul to rest.

Gayle approached the casket and put her hand on the pillow that held Meisha's head. The mortician had done an excellent job reconstructing her facial features and the mutilated tissue around the base of her neck. One of the bullets struck her directly at the top of her spine. Another hit her in the chest, and the other blew off a portion of her face.

Gayle was afraid to touch Meisha, but she was not afraid to tell her that she loved her. Leaning over into the casket, she whispered into her daughter's fallen ears all of the pain and all of the love that she knew only God could have cursed upon her. This was His punishment for what she had done to Chris. But from this pain and love, a song came, more beautiful than any love ballad, more spiritual than any amazing grace. It was the only heartfelt song she had ever sung, for it was a song from a mother to her child.

The only things that moved were the gates of heaven.

After her solo, Gayle rushed outside hoping for the chance to talk to Sheila before the family cars left. She thought about all the evil things that she had said to Chris while she stood there. She thought about the last words that Chris had spoken to her. Then she felt someone touch her shoulder.

"That was really a beautiful job you did in there," a woman's voice said quietly.

"Thank you," she said politely.

"Sounded like you knew her."

"I did once. She was my baby."

"Yeah, Meisha was everybody's baby. Don't be sad. She forgives you for everything."

"She never knew who I was." Gayle turned around and saw no one, but still felt a presence. Then the wind whispered, "Yes, she did."

Although she saw Gayle standing there, Sheila never stopped by the tree, but Gayle realized that they hadn't spoken in these many years. Why even start? Some things were better left unspoken.

▲

Late that night Gayle needed companionship. She called Monica and got no answer. So she paged her and waited for the return call. It was almost an hour later.

"Did you page me?" Monica snapped.

"Yes, I did," Gayle responded solemnly. "Are you busy?"

"Kinda. What you want?" Monica, since Gayle had known her, never showed any kind of compassion toward her. She was what Chris called "an-around-the-way" girl. Monica knew of Gayle's reputation and gave her basically what she deserved—rudeness, insensitivity, and a cold shoulder. "You musta wanted something, calling me this late."

"Nothing, Never mind. I was just calling 'cause I hadn't heard from you today." It was then she realized that she needed Chris, and paying a visit to her in the hospital wasn't such a bad idea after all.

"Well, aiight then," Monica responded as she slammed the phone down. She wanted Gayle to chase her, and she wanted her to leave that uppity bitch, Chris, alone. In the church community, Monica was considered a choir groupie and lusted after the reigning divas of the scene. She was definitely full of herself and full of the games that Gayle had once played. Younger than Gayle, Monica had time to create those games, to manipulate those games, and to win at those games. After tonight, Gayle had decided that it was time to retire her jersey. No more games.

▲

It was two o'clock in the morning, and Gayle was wide awake. Visiting hours didn't start until ten. She had eight hours to get her shit together. Reaching for her purse, she tried to remember the name of the elder at church that was in charge of the twenty-four-hour prayer line. Damn, what was his name? The night after Chris ran her off the road, she had to sing at a banquet and that was where she'd met him. They talked for hours, and he picked up that she was troubled about something but refused to admit that she needed help. He worked for the city and had crazy hours. What was his name! She found his card stuck between the Book of Exodus and the church bulletin. Twenty-fours, huh.

"Memphis Fire Department."

What? The Fire Department? She knew she must have dialed the wrong number and hung up the phone. She dialed the number again.

"Memphis Fire Department."

"I'm sorry. I must keep dialing the wrong phone number."

"Well, who are you looking for?"

"Uh, one of my church members. He gave me this number and…"

"Hold on, the man you want is right here."

There was a long pause before someone picked up the receiver. "Murphy, can I help you?"

"Elder Murphy, this is…"

"I know who it is. How you doing, Sister Evans?"

"Not too good tonight, I'm afraid."

"Well, tell me what's on your heart, Sister."

Gayle poured her heart out to Elder Murphy for over two hours. She cried and begged for forgiveness. She asked God to make everything right and to put it upon Chris' heart to forgive her. Mr. Murphy stopped her and thought for a minute.

"Chris? Is that the name of the woman that you've been telling me about?'

"Yes, it is. Why?"

"It was my rig that picked her up that morning. She was in a real bad way."

"Wait a minute. She really did try to kill herself?"

"She almost did. Praise God that she got help in time."

Gayle was dumbfounded. "I thought that she was lying. I thought she just checked herself in there to get some attention from me. I mean, I…Oh, God, what have I done?"

"Um, she wasn't playing, but if it makes you feel any better, she's doing extremely well."

"How do you know?"

"Well, after she had been in the hospital for a few days and after getting some assessments done, she called our church looking for Patrick, of all people. But he'd just left. I remembered who she was, and I told her who I was. At first she was hesitant but she eventually went ahead and told me her story. The most wonderful thing that she told me was that she had found God since she'd been in the hospital."

"Excuse me?" Gayle was in shock.

"You know the story of Nebuchadnezzar and how God sent him into the wilderness and made him go stone crazy until he had realized that he needed God in his life?"

"Not really familiar with it, but I've heard sermons on it."

"Well, after days and days of being out there in the wild, he finally believed. He accepted our Lord God. And that's what has happened to her. After that, I took Patrick out there with me, since he's still in training. He has really taken to her."

"You're talking about Patty Bennett, right?" Gayle had to get clarification because she knew that there was bad blood between Patty and Chris.

"Yes, I am. When his mother passed, some of his ways died, too. He even broke up with his friend. Patty mentioned to me that, despite the fact that he and Chris didn't get along, he was really sorry for all she was going through and wanted her to know that he understood. Their mutual dislike for each other is in the past now."

That explained why no one had seen Patrick in over two weeks. His mother died in her sleep the same night that Chris had tried to commit suicide. Gayle realized that through all of the songs she had directed and sung and through all the arguments about religion that she and Chris had experienced, the soul that He was after was really Chris'. He had taken the lives of Meisha and Mrs. Bennett to get to the soul of one of his lost children. Patty and Chris finally had become friends through the eyes of God.

"As a matter of fact, Gayle, Chris came to one of our evening services. She really didn't have much of a reaction to it though. Since Patrick got his calling from the Lord, he's been there pretty regularly himself."

"Has she joined yet?"

"Naw, not yet."

"She probably won't. That girl doesn't have a religious bone in her body."

"She may not be religious, but she's one of the most spiritual people I know. She told me about how much she despised the bishop and she told me why. She also mentioned something to me about that sermon he did on the fullness of time. She regurgitated that entire sermon to me. I explained to her that it had been the devil working to keep her away from God. Then she explained that she could not be a child of God and be gay at the same time. I agreed. But not without first telling her that He created her like that because He knew that she had it in her to be delivered from it. It may not be today or tomorrow or next week or next month, but she and you both will be delivered."

"So you're saying it's wrong?"

"Gayle, you're the Minister of Music who has more skeletons in her closet than the graveyard has bones. You know what's in the Bible, and so does she."

"Well, I was going to stop by to see her in the morning."

"Don't."

"Why not?"

"Because she needs this time alone. Let me share something with you. I'm telling you this because there's nothing too powerful for God. I told you about those things that concern the both of you. You both have some of the same problems, but they come from different sides of reality. She has faced hers and, now, I encourage you to do the same."

Her heart was so heavy that she could hardly move. She couldn't say another word because she was finally confronted with her issues and those issues almost destroyed a life.

"I guess you think I'm a pretty bad person after all this. I mean, now that you know the truth and everything."

"You're human, Gayle, and there's nothing any of us can do about that. You know something?"

"What?"

"Do you know what drove her to do all the things she did?"

"No, I guess not since you're bringing it up."

"You used God in your deception. You looked Him right in the face and spit on Him. You took your lies and your deceit and played on Chris' empathy about religion. And that's what destroyed her, and it has also taken its toll on you." It was just after seven, and his shift was over. "I'll see you in church on Sunday, Sister Evans. I hope that I get to hear you sing."

22

Chris was discharged from the hospital because she was an extremely good actress. "I guess if I eat a little something they'll move me out of the crazy room," she said to herself. So she picked at two meals, eating only the bread and vegetables, and they moved her into a new wing with fewer restrictions. "If I interact in group discussions, they'll let me go home." So she started participating. She made some of the most severely depressed people laugh for the first time in months. She kept her Bible with her at all times, talked with Elder Murphy and Darcy every day, and most importantly, she talked with God.

It was He who had given her the strength to face the day, and it was He who helped her to confront her issues. Chris knew that she was going to survive. The first stop she made was to her mother's house to see her babies. In her heart there was so much love for them that it overflowed into her eyes. They couldn't talk back to her, but she felt that they understood why she had to do the things she had done. She had grown to realize that there is no love stronger than the one between mother and child. Their love for her was unconditional, and no matter how many women came and went, they would always be right there for her.

"Momma," she said quietly with tears in her eyes. It was the first time in several months that she had sat down with her mother to talk. There wasn't a knot in her chest, nor was there any guilt in her soul.

"Yes, baby, what is it?"

"It's time for us to go. Me and my babies."

Ms. Desmereaux looked at her daughter and tried to understand where this was going. "Chris, baby, you just got out of the hospital and..."

"I know, Momma, but, after all that has happened here in this town, I need to go. I have to go."

"Honey, I have plenty of space here for y'all. I understand that you do the things you do because that's what you want. I don't understand it, but I have to accept it because you're my child. I'm not going to bother you. I..."

Chris stood up and got some tissue from the bathroom. "Momma, do you actually think that I choose to be this way? Loving women and being emotionally attached to them? I want to have a big society wedding with all the trimmings and stuff. I want to be married to a man, but my heart just isn't there. It would be so unfair to some woman's son for me to lead him on when I truly know that I could never love him as it is written that a wife should. All I know is that God has given me the strength to get my life in order so that I might be a mother to my children. He has given me the strength to deal with my sexuality in such a way that suits Him...not you, not Daddy, and not even me. I'm tired of always needing some-body. I needed Trey to help me with Chelsea, and he left. I needed Gayle for a lot of things, and she left, too. The both of them left me in so much need that I had to step back and take a look at myself. You didn't raise me to depend on anybody. I'm not that kind of a person. The only person that I need in my life right now has been there with me all the time, and I've been too stupid to even know it. Right now, I just want to and need to be alone."

"Where are you going to go, Chrissie?"

"Darcy just moved to Philadelphia, and her place is big enough for me and the girls. The probation office is helping me get a transfer to an office up there. I'll stay with the office long enough to save up some money for my own place. Next spring, I'm going to start working on my Masters degree at Temple. I'll be all right, Momma. I'll be all right, as long as I don't have to be here."

"Have you spoken to that girl?"

"No, I haven't. I've been spending a lot of time at church, trying to get myself together."

"Church?" Ms. Desmereaux was shocked.

"Don't worry. I haven't bought a tambourine just yet." Chris laughed. "I have found that there's a lot more to it than that."

Staring at her grandbabies and their mother, Ms. Desmereaux knew that leaving the city was the best thing for her child. Ever since she'd left Chris in D.C. during her freshman year at Howard, she'd known that Chris wasn't a true country girl. She blended in with those uppity colored folks, like she'd been born and raised around them. Ms. Desmereaux knew that this time she had to let go. "Let me know if you need anything. I know that I haven't been the mother that you needed me to be, and I'm sorry for that. I probably should've kept my mouth shut about your business. Maybe a lot of this wouldn't have happened. I just wish that you would've tried to come to me."

"Momma, I don't regret anything that happened." Pointing to the sky, she said, "It was His way of telling me that I needed to get it together."

Wiping her eyes, she told Chris, "You better take care of my babies! They look just like you, and I know that they love you to death!" Ms. Desmereaux held Gaylon while Chris put Chelsea in her car seat. "You need to take special care of this one," she said as she handed the baby to Chris. "She's gonna need you more than you'll ever know."

Chris turned to her mother and hugged her. It was the first hug that they had shared since Chris had been back in Memphis. "I'm gonna leave tomorrow, but I need to get the girls some things for the road. You know where I'm going for that, don't you?"

Her mother smiled. "Wal-Mart."

"You wanna ride with us?" Chris gave her mother the biggest smile.

Ms. Desmereaux hurriedly got into the car with her daughter…for old time's sake. As they headed across the Tennessee state line into Southaven, Mississippi, Chris took her mother's hand and said, "I love you, Momma. I really do."

▲

Sara had been bedridden for almost fifteen years. She had no desire to be rehabilitated; refusing therapy and anything else that would help her get better. On the weekends, Sadie stayed with her to feed her, bathe her, and provide company for her. Gayle had reneged on her promise to watch Sara and was never at home. On holidays, she'd stopped by to eat and to spend a couple of minutes with her aunt—the only real mother she'd ever had.

This particular weekend she'd been with Patty and Monica. Because it kept going off while they were kissing and playing around, Monica took Gayle's pager and hid it under the bed. It had a code 9-1-1 in it and, from previous experiences, Monica just knew that it was nobody but Chris. Yeah, they fucked that night but, for Gayle, Monica had purely become just "something to do."

When Gayle got up that Sunday morning, she realized that she'd forgotten her shoes for church. In spite of being a community choir groupie, Monica was not a churchgoer. She told Gayle that she could drive her car on to church since Patty had to be there so early. "I can drive my own car. Thank you, though." But when she got outside, the car wouldn't crank. Gayle looked at the dashboard and saw that a door had been left open. DAMN!

Gayle hadn't been home in a couple of days and, for some reason, she wanted to see Sara's face. Although she had no motor skills, her cognitive functions were somewhat intact. Words like "no," "stop," and even a chuckle sometimes were the only movements of her mouth. Today Gayle wanted to touch Sara and hold her. In all the years of her illness, Gayle had wanted to say so many things, but she'd never had the courage. On this Sunday morning, Gayle was ready, for Sara was the only person who would understand Gayle's never-ending love for Chris.

Hearing her fumbling with her keys, Sadie opened the door. "You finally decided to come home," she said as she walked away.

"I forgot my shoes for church." The house didn't smell like it usually did on Sundays. There were no greens, no cakes or pies. "Are you not cooking today?" Gayle yelled toward her aunt's room while heading toward the hall closet. "Sadie, you hear me?" There was no answer.

Walking toward Sara's room, she didn't hear a sound. No television, no movement. The room was empty. Gayle ran through the house looking for Sadie. As she passed the hallway, she saw the basement door open. Down the stairs, a light was on, and someone was down there moving things around. "Where's Sara?" she asked.

Sadie was packing some clothes in a trunk. The entire basement reeked of mothballs. Never making eye contact with her daughter, she neatly folded sheets and blouses. "Why didn't you answer your pager? I beeped your ass for two days straight!"

"I was kinda tied up. Where's Sara?"

"We decided to put her in a nursing home," she said carelessly. "Next time, maybe you'll be responsible and answer a page."

"What!"

"Hell, you're never here to help take care of her. I can't even get you to watch over her on the weekends so I can try to have a life for a change. And you ain't even doing shit most of the time 'cept for lying up under that nasty ass girl."

"Who the hell is we?"

"Don't worry about it. She's gone. You and yo' grown ass ain't never been here 'cept to eat and flaunt yo' trashy ass friends around us. It wasn't fair to the rest of us, Gayle. I mean, after all, ain't you supposed to be her daughter anyway?"

"Oh, okay, I see. That's what this is all about. You jealous, ain't you?"

"No, I'm not. Have you ever bothered to ask me why you been living here all these years?"

"Nope, because I knew why. You didn't want me. But you turned around and had more children and kept them all with you."

"See, that's why you all fucked up in the head. You don't think. I gave you to Sara because she could give you what I couldn't at the time. All I could give you was a gov'ment check and some food stamps. What kind of life is that to give a child? I wish you could've seen the look in yo' eyes whenever I came to pick you up. You wanted to stay with Sara. I wanted you to be happy, Gayle. I wanted my sister to be happy. She couldn't have any kids of her own, and…"

"Wait a minute! Junior ain't her son?"

"Girl, naw, he and his daddy ain't even related to us. They just friends of the family. Anyway, she wanted you, and you wanted to be with her. I did what was best for everybody." Sadie stood there thinking. "Why you ask me about Junior and Bo?"

After years of silence, Gayle knew it was time for that hush to be broken. "You remember the Sunday after my prom? The day that you stopped by to leave some food over here?"

Sadie glared at the wall for a minute and looked at Gayle. "Yeah, I do."

"Bo and Junior…they raped me that day."

Sadie covered her mouth and gasped. The memories of that day came rushing from the past. She immediately remembered her firstborn's demeanor that day and, unlike the first time, she listened as Gayle told her the details. "That's why you asked me could you come home." Tears filled the wells of her eyes. She pulled Gayle to her bosom. "I'm so sorry, honey. Why didn't you say something then?"

Crying tears of shame, Gayle whimpered, "I tried to, but you didn't give me a chance. I gave my baby away because of that. I did love her, Momma. I wanted to keep my baby, but I…"

"Shhh, you don't have to say no mo'. Now, I understand."

23

The last thing Chris wanted to do was to have to come back to Memphis for something, so she spent all night going through her mother's house collecting her and the children's belongings. She gave away all of the furnishings that she and Gayle had accumulated and only kept the things that belonged to the children. It was a beautiful Sunday morning to travel but, before she left, there was something that she had to do.

"Chris! Hey, Chris, wait up!" It was about seven-thirty, and folks were already packing in. Elder Murphy caught up with Chris and walked her to the building. "I got your message. When are you leaving?"

"After service."

"This one?"

"No, I'm gonna try all three today."

"What! Not you, Miss 'I ain't sittin' through all of that'?"

"Yeah, that was me back in the day. I've changed. The babies and I are outta here after the noon service." She looked around, as if she were expecting someone.

John knew what was up. "She's not here yet."

"Have you talked to her?"

"Yes, as a matter of fact, I have, and I think that you should, too. She could learn a lot from you right now."

"That's not such a good idea. Things are best as they are." She noticed the line of people waiting to get into the parking lot. "Let me go and get me a seat. I ain't as fortunate as you to have a reserved spot right up front." She laughed. "Give me a hug, my friend." John hugged her and, for the first time in his life, he let a woman see him cry.

The first service was usually more constrained than the second and third ones. The last service was most crowded because, like Chris, the bishop's followers stayed with him all day long. Chairs filled the aisles in the noon service, the balcony was full and so was the east wing of the sanctuary.

There was a little time before service started, and Chris decided to go to the rest room while everybody was still engaged in fellowship outside. When she came out of the stall, she walked right into Gayle. "Did you follow me in here?"

"Well, I kinda waited for you to get up. I saw you from the pulpit. I didn't know that you were coming in here."

"How are you?" Chris asked hesitantly. She couldn't believe that Gayle had the gall to sit in the pulpit after everything that had happened. Well, yes, she could.

"I'm all right. And you?"

"Beautiful. Simply beautiful. I heard about your daughter."

"Yeah, I thought you might." She looked her watch. "I really need to talk to you."

"About what? We've said all that we need to say to each other. I think that we should leave it at that."

"So..." Gayle paused as the last person left the room. "You still messing around? I mean, you know?"

Chris laughed. "I can't say that I am, and I can't say that I am not. I'm just being me right now."

"Well, I know what that means." Gayle noticed something about Chris' demeanor. She was pleasantly calm and seemed not to have a care in the world. "I'm stepping down today. You know, after all that's happened. I told the bishop that this would be my last Sunday."

"You probably should." Chris seemed to have no remorse for Gayle.

"You wanna know why I really left you and the kids?"

"Not really."

"C'mon, Chris. I'm serious."

"Me, too, but if it's gonna make you feel better, shoot your best shot."

Clearing her throat, Gayle took a seat on a nearby stool. "I left before you had a chance to leave me. I mean, everybody that I've ever really loved has left me. Sadie. Sara. Meisha. No warning, nothing. I know that I'm not one of the best people in the world. If I just had a chance…"

"Wait a minute. You had a chance, and you blew it. Life is too short to blow it on chances. I would have never left you, and you know that. You didn't trust our love the way I did. Everything about you was learned from someone other than you. Gay or not, my love was there for you…for us. I almost sacrificed my babies for you, Gayle! How much more love do you need from one person?"

"Chris, I'm sorry. Truly I am. Being away from you all this time has made me realize how much you mean to me and just how much I need you."

"No, you don't. I promise you that you don't, but you want to know something?"

"I'm afraid to say I do."

"Don't be. You remember how you always wanted me to hear you sing?"

"Yeah, but you never did."

Chris chuckled. "You see, you're wrong. I've heard you sing, and so many emotions ran through my body when I did. I was filled with envy and heartache all at the same time. I was jealous because I wished that I could sing like that, and my heart was broken because God gave you a voice that's obviously supposed to bring joy to the most desolate person, but all you use it for is to soothe your overinflated ego and to try to redeem your sins on Sunday mornings. Have you ever wondered why your singing doesn't take you where you want to go with it?"

A tearful Gayle said nothing.

"It's because you're not doing what He wants you to do with it. I see that with my own life. Nothing was going right because I'd been doing everything except what I'm supposed to be doing. I know who I am now, and you know, it's not such a bad thing." While turning to walk out of the rest room, she noticed Gayle's keys—the keys to that blue Honda. Some people never change, she thought. "The girls and I are leaving today. We've got to get out of this city. If you want any of that stuff we had, it's at the Salvation Army. It was all stolen anyway."

Gayle moved closer to Chris and placed her hand upon Chris' shoulder. "You don't want to try to save what we had?"

Then Chris remembered and repeated what Carlos had once said to her. "Gayle, some things aren't worth being saved."

"So you're going to walk away from us, just like that?"

As the organ began to softly play, Chris looked out into the sanctuary and smiled. "One of us has to."

▲

The choir was especially beautiful that morning with Gayle's direction more powerful than ever before. Following her performance the bishop took the pulpit and preached his sermon from the book of Daniel, speaking about the deliverance of Shadrach, Meshach, and Abednego from the fiery furnace. He spoke to Chris about deliverance from the fire. As he extended the invitation, the bishop requested that Gayle sing a hymn that she had sung so well so many times before. With a nod of the head, the musicians began "When Sunday Comes."

As the organ trilled, a hum so soft drifted over the sanctuary that everyone who heard it was moved with a feeling of indescribable joy. A heartfelt hum that grew to a low moan filled with all the pain she carried deep within the crevices of her soul, a pain that no one, not even Chris, knew was there. With eyes squeezed shut and hands tightly clenched, slowly Gayle began to sing the words that had moved so many of God's children countless times before. For the first time as she sang them, the words moved Gayle as well.

"When Sunday comes, my trouble's gone. As soon as it gets here, I'll have a new song. I won't have to cry no more. Jesus will soothe my troubled mind. All of my heartaches will be left behind, when Sunday comes."

With every note she sang, with every tear that fell, God's presence ripped through everyone who heard. His spirit was in them, their feet, their bodies, and their souls. As they wrapped their arms around themselves, slowing swaying from side to side rocking back and forth, their rhythmic tapping told all He was there. And they answered. "Thank you, Lord! Yes, Jesus! My Lord! My God! You've been so good! Thank you, Jesus! Thank you!" It resonated from the oldest member of the Mother's board, proudly sitting on the front pew next to the altar, to the youngest of the visitors tucked "safely" away on the last seat at the back of the church.

"Just to behold His face, His saving grace. Oh yes, I've got to see Jesus for me when Sunday comes."

And for Chris it had. Her soul was on fire with a quivering in her chest, pounding and thumping begging for release. Beginning as a flutter but increasing intensely with each passing second, it raced from the tips of her toes to the longest ends of her well-manicured nails. Chris gasped at this feeling; she struggled to inhale. This feeling. What is it? "A gnawing," her mother had called it the day Jesus had pulled her back into the fold. "Once It gets in you child, ain't no way you can get out." Chris felt it move within her, this fire she couldn't explain. Her mother had always said there were two ways to burn. "To purify or destroy, Chris. To purify or destroy."

That day in the sanctuary, God was cleansing Chris' tattered soul, rejuvenating her with an abundance of His ever-merciful love. The floors of the church were vibrating. His spirit was busy healing. Every arm was raised to the heavens. Every mind filled with thoughts of salvation. Each eye shedding tears of joy.

"Excuse me, excuse me," Chris pleaded as she stepped over the people standing next to her. "Please, please, let me out! I've got to get out! Please, Jesus, let me out!" she cried.

Chris made it to the aisle and let the Holy Spirit move through her. She danced. She cried. For the first time in her life, Chris praised the Lord. There was no shame; there was no restraint. Holding back never even entered her mind. The congregation supported her, cheering her on and softly touching her hand or shoulder as she moved past every pew.

And there, at the altar, she fell upon her knees and accepted the Lord's invitation.

▲

"Then they cried unto the Lord in their trouble, and he saved them out of their distresses. He brought them out of darkness and the shadow of death, and brake their bands in sunder."
—*Psalms 107: 13-14*

EXCERPT FROM THE FORTHCOMING NOVEL

UnderCover

BY LAURINDA D. BROWN

COMING OCTOBER 2004

Miss Nay's Revue

Patrick sat at the bar waiting for the love of his life. The house was packed as usual with folks in from Atlanta and St. Louis for the holiday weekend. Cars were lined up on both sides of Front Street that night—which wasn't a big deal to many. But, to Patrick, it meant the world.

It meant that everyone had come out to see his baby perform at the club. Men from all walks of life handed Patrick's lady dollar bills, five-dollar bills, ten-dollar bills, and, on the first of the month, maybe even some twenties. But none could surpass Patrick. Every Saturday night, dressed to the nines, he would watch those other men walk to the front of the stage and place bills in his lady's hand. They often tripped over themselves to do it, and some even borrowed from their dates just to touch the silken hands of The Menagerie's biggest star. But it was Patrick who made a hush fall over the crowded room. Leaving his double B-52 and Lite Beer, he would get up from his table and reach into his pocket. He was so smooth that the air around seemed to stand still. With every stride—waving that bill in his hand, eyes followed him, wondering what he'd pulled from that pocket. By the time he reached the stage, the bill was creased across Ben Franklin's face and gently rested on his index finger. And Miss Nay? She would simply lean over and smile as he placed the crisp one hundred-dollar bill between her breasts.

Tonight, though, Patrick was not all right. He didn't get his usual table in the center of the dance floor. Instead, he sat at the bar and nursed a flat ginger ale that had succumbed to the two cubes of ice that the bartender so graciously offered. Tonight he hadn't even bothered to remove this jacket because he knew that he wouldn't be staying long. "Patty, wanna 'notha drink?" someone offered. But Patrick remained silent and kept swirling his straw around the bottom of his glass. "Guess not," as the waitress made her way to the other end of the bar. Patrick stoically sat there with his back turned to the stage. The air around him was so cold that passersby just kept their distance. Three years seemed like only three days to Patty, for he and Miss Nay were lovers at first sight. The two of them had shared such an intense love during their courtship that not a single soul dared to cross the line. As she performed, Miss Nay electrified the crowd with her sultry moves and finesse. Nay was off limits, though, to the rest of the club and sometimes even to the rest of the world. Everybody knew that. That was the way Patrick wanted it.

Patrick, with not a harsh bone in his body, dropped his head in agony and closed his eyes. With the music so loud, no one could hear him thinking out loud. "Nay, Baby, you know that I love you. I love you more than I ever imagined I could. Whenever we're together, nothing else in this world has ever mattered to me, but I've reached a point in my life where some things have come to matter to me. The things that I chose to turn the other cheek to have come around and smacked me in the face. I can't continue to act like the world around me is just grand when my insides are about to fall out. You see, baby, since my mama died, I've been going to church, and I kinda like it. I mean, it's like my soul just opens up when I'm there. All these people around me… hundreds of them, and, with all that, I still feel like it's just me and God. When I go there, baby, I like what I see. I like what I hear." Even at octaves above a whisper at times, it seemed as if no one had heard a word Patty had said. He continued, "Nay, I realize now that love is more than what we have. It's more that what I ever thought we had. The last thing that I've ever wanted to do was to hurt you, but, after all these months of Sunday School, Bible study, and worship services, I now know that life is about the choices you make, and right now… today, I choose God."

Patty's heart was so full of emotion that tears were pouring down his face. But, you see, time was still, for at that moment, he thought there was no one else in the room but him and God; however, when Patty opened his eyes, there was also Miss Nay.

This epitome of refined elegance and style exemplified regal stature yet this woman of grandeur, this mega diva worthy of applause until her last breath, simply sat there with her now former lover, and shed the same tears. She shared the pain. The once flawless makeup was now smeared revealing the mustache fuzz and facial hair. Nay, displaying divine class and composure to the end, slowly removed the silk scarf that was a gift from Patty. Speechless, Nay reached for Patty's cheek and gently kissed it. Afterwards, she draped the scarf around Patty's neck and sauntered toward the door.

Once out that door, it would be the first time in years that she would have to face the world as Nathaniel Buford.

About the Author

A native of Memphis, Tennessee and a graduate of
Howard University's English Department, Laurinda
believes in divine destiny. "When you do what your passion
is—your passion being what God gave you the zest
and talent to do—the rest falls into place."

Laurinda D. Brown writes about life...not lifestyles.